SUBTERRANEA

P.K. HAWKINS

SEVERED PRESS
HOBART TASMANIA

SUBTERRANEA

Copyright © 2020 Severed Press

WWW.SEVEREDPRESS.COM

ISBN: 978-1-922323-38-5

PROLOGUE

The facility's klaxons continued to blare even after the horror was over, and Special Agent Larson was forced to run into the project's main control room, her gun still drawn, and demand answers.

"I thought you idiots said the thing was shut down!"

"We did!" one of the main scientists said from his control panel, which seemed to be smoking and sparking. "It is! But the readings seem to indicate that it's going to open again within the hour."

"Then the general will just have to get more soldiers and be prepared for another breach."

"But Agent Larson, that's the problem," the scientist said. "The readings don't say anything about the portal opening again here. The monitors seem to indicate a spike of energy outside the facility."

Larson's jaw dropped. "That's not supposed to be possible at this stage."

"And yet that's exactly what seems to be happening," the scientist said. His tone seemed to suggest that somehow he seemed to think this was all her fault. Just let him think that, then. Everyone blamed her for everything that went wrong around here anyway, even when it was very blatantly the fault of that idiot general.

"Where then?" Larson asked. "Please at least tell me it's going to happen in some corn field somewhere that no one is using at this time of year."

The scientist gave a series of coordinates as they appeared on the glowing green screen of his computer. Special Agent Larson thought about them for a moment, comparing them to what she knew about this region, then swore loud and long.

"What's so bad about that?" another scientist asked. "Isn't that the middle of nowhere?"

"It is, but it just so happens to be one of the few spots in that area with people in it." She started to run out of the room, then called out to the scientists over her shoulder as she left. "Someone tell the general. There's a very small town out there that is about to experience a very big heap of trouble."

CHAPTER ONE

With a total population of six hundred and twenty-four people, Kettle Hollow, Wisconsin barely registered on most maps. Its biggest claim to fame was that it was the home town of a player who had briefly been a part of the 1982 Milwaukee Brewers line-up, but an injury had ended his career pretty quickly and now, three years later, none of the townsfolk even knew where he lived anymore. There was parochial school as part of the Catholic church, but otherwise all the schoolchildren had to be bused over to Sheboygan. There was a diner and a gas station near the center of town, and near the edge of town (which, quite frankly, was only a block or so from the center) there was a Piggly Wiggly grocery store and a mom and pop pharmacy. That was it. That was pretty much every major landmark in the town that wasn't somebody's house.

It did have a single stoplight although as the darkness of the early autumn night fell over the town, that stoplight's time left on Earth was to be measured in hours rather than days.

At the outskirts of the town and in the farm fields that surrounded it, whispers could be heard by anyone listening, along with the occasional soft squawk of a walkie-talkie. But the forces gathering out there were still unsure that their greatest fear was about to happen, so they resisted descending on the town just yet, hoping that the early warning they'd been given was a false alarm.

Beyond that perimeter of hiding figures, in a rock quarry off a mostly deserted county road, four much younger people were making a lot more noise, or at least three of them were. Maureen "Murky" Lensky proved to be the quietest of the four, mostly because at eleven she was the youngest and felt like she didn't belong with the others. She was the only one riding an old 70's Schwinn while the other three had BMXs of various brands. None of them encouraged her to join in as they practiced dangerous stunts (or at least dangerous in the minds of twelve and thirteen-year-olds). She wouldn't even be here if her mother had forced her thirteen-year old sister Laura to bring her along. Their mom had said it was because Murky didn't get out of the house enough, but Murky had understood the silent look her mother had given her just as she was leaving the house. Murky's real reason for being out here was because their mother didn't trust Laura alone with Henderson.

Henderson's real name was George Patrick Staude. No one knew why he called himself Henderson, and anyone who tried to call him by his given name tended to walk away with bruises or black eyes. He was hardly a large person, but people tended to avoid him. Murky wouldn't exactly consider him a bully, but he made little to no attempt to make friends. He wore faded flannel shirts and torn jeans because his family couldn't afford much else, and in order to prevent others from making fun of him for this he tried to take on an intimidating air. Murky's mother thought he was a bad influence, but he was never mean to Murky. If anything, he was rather protective of her because she was Laura's sister, and wherever Laura went, he followed.

At this exact moment he was trying to precariously balance his BMX on an outcropping of rock. He'd been that way for several minutes now, declaring that as soon as he was ready he would pull off some kind of amazing trick. Laura waited patiently nearby with her own Huffy BMX while the fourth member of their group, Jesse, jeered up at him.

"Hey Henderson, it's okay to admit you're a chicken!" he said. Jesse was the only one who could talk to Henderson like that without getting punched in the face. Part of that was probably because he wore thick glasses, and Henderson knew what kind of hell Jesse's parents would rain down on him if he broke them. Murky thought a bigger part of it though, was that Jesse always let Henderson copy his homework, and in exchange Henderson acted as the wiry, smart-ass kid's pseudo bodyguard. "Who knows? Maybe even Team Murray is looking for a chicken to join them next time they compete in the Olympics. Gotta have a mascot, right?"

"Team Murray doesn't compete in the Olympics, you numbnuts," Henderson said with noticeable anger in his voice. While Murky didn't have their same obsession with dirt bikes, even she knew better than to insult Henderson's great dream of someday racing his bike professionally. "Keep it up Jesse, and when I land, I'll do it right on your head!" Henderson said.

"That would require you to jump your bike down here first; at this rate I'll already be in bed by the time you do that!"

"Speaking of bed, it's getting pretty late," Laura said. "My mom's going to get angry if we stay out here too much longer. It's a school night."

"Like I care," Henderson muttered, but as was usually the case, when Laura spoke to him reasonably, he listened. Murky was sure her mother thought Laura and Henderson were probably sneaking out to make-out, but she could see that Laura was more like the mother Henderson didn't have. Murky didn't yet know the word "platonic," but if she did that was exactly how she would have described that relationship.

"Wait, we can't go yet," Murky said. "I haven't seen any of the bats come out. There's supposed to be a whole bunch of them that live around here." Even as she said it though, she went to grab her backpack from where she had dumped it along with the others. Regardless of whether or not she was ready, she'd learned long ago not to mess with Laura when she was in mother hen mode.

"Bleh!" Jesse said as he grabbed his backpack as well. "Bats are gross. That's seriously the main reason you wanted to come out here with us?"

Murky shrugged. She was used to others not getting her. Even Laura didn't seem to understand her, even though Laura would defend her with her life. "I just like bats."

"You like every animal, Murky," Laura said. All four of them had their backpacks again, but rather than immediately riding back they walked their bikes out of the quarry. Despite Laura's admonishment, none of them were exactly in a hurry to get back home.

"Not *every* animal," Murky said defensively.

"Name one animal that you don't like," Henderson said.

"Uh, those one things."

Jesse gave an obnoxious snort of a laugh. "Those one things. Is that supposed to be the scientific name?"

"Spiders," Murky said, naming the first plausible creature that came to mind."

"Try again," Laura said. "I caught you playing with that disgusting spider egg sack last week."

"Fine. Uh. Mr. Turnbull."

They all had a good hard laugh at that. Mr. Turnbull was the old man who ran the pharmacy.

Despite being one of the few places in town where they could get comics and magazines and candy, no one actually liked going in there. Mr. Turnbull was cranky and smelled like hemorrhoid cream.

"Is your mom really going to be mad if you guys are home this late?" Henderson asked Laura.

"Probably."

Henderson shook his head. "Must be nice."

"Why is it nice that Mom would get mad at us?" Murky asked.

"I mean, must be nice having parents that care enough to even *be* mad," Henderson said. He refused to look at any of them as he spoke.

"Man, your dad just lets you run around and do whatever you want," Jesse said. "We all wish we had *your* dad."

Murky wasn't sure if Henderson looked like he would rather cry or smack Jesse right across the mouth. Personally, Murky would definitely take the relationship she had with her own parents over what Henderson had. She knew that his mother had been killed in a workplace accident when Henderson was little, and his father had started drinking after that. She didn't think he did anything to hurt Henderson, but sometimes she wondered if Henderson would have preferred that to being treated like he didn't even exist.

From somewhere out in a field at the side of the road, Murky heard some kind of electronic squawk. She stopped to listen, but because she was trailing behind the others it took them a moment to realize she was no longer following.

"Come on, Murky. We don't have a lot of time left."

"Didn't you guys hear that?" Murky asked.

"I didn't hear nothing," Henderson said.

They all stood quietly for second. At first Murky thought that maybe it had been her imagination, but with everyone quiet now she thought she could also hear the rustle of something large moving through the tall brown grass.

"Probably an animal," Laura said. "No, you can't go see what it is. You'll probably bring it home, and Mom will kill me if I let you bring home any more strays."

Before Murky could protest, she felt a slight rumble in the road. She'd walked and ridden on these county roads enough to expect it to be some kind of truck coming by, but when she looked up and down the road it was completely empty. Come to think of it, they hadn't seen *any* traffic going toward or away from town since they left the quarry. While there certainly wasn't any reason for outsiders to visit Kettle Hollow, this particular road was sometimes used as a shortcut by people trying to get to more lively places. There should have been *something* during this time, and yet there hadn't been.

"Do you guys feel that?" Jesse asked. "It feels like the whole world is vibrating."

Down the road they could see the lights in the houses at the edge of town suddenly go out, and the vibrating increased until Murky could feel it in her bones.

"Something's…"

Murky could only assume that Laura was about to say "Something's wrong," but the last word was ripped from her mouth by a sudden boom accompanied with a flash of light from the direction of the center of Kettle Hollow.

And that wasn't even the most alarming thing that happened during the next couple of seconds. While they were all turned to the blinding flash, multiple soldiers erupted out from various hiding places in the fields around them, and the night became full of shouted commands. Most of the soldiers took positions with their weapons pointed to the town, like they thought a sudden attack might come from the sleepy little village. Three of them though, ran right to the kids.

"Don't move!" a soldier yelled at them. "Hands where we can see them!"

Murky immediately dropped her bike and put her hands up like she'd seen in movies. Laura and Jesse did the same, although Henderson hesitated. He looked like he wanted to punch the soldier for threatening him, or maybe he was just hesitant to drop his prized bike, even if it was a cheap knock-off of the Murray X20C he actually wanted. Thankfully he did as he was told.

While soldiers surrounded them, the flashing from town stopped, although a low rumble continued to be heard. Murky also thought she might have heard screaming, but she hoped that was just her imagination.

One of the soldiers took out a walkie-talkie and spoke into it. "Sir, we've got a problem at Checkpoint H. It looks like four of the kids from the town weren't in it as the portal erupted."

"Damn it!" a voice on the other end said. "We

don't have time for this. Detain them and take them back to the base camp. We can make that Larson woman babysit them while we do our jobs."

"Roger that." The soldier put away the walkie-talkie and then gestured at the kids with his weapon. "Come on. This way."

"What… what's happening?" Laura asked. "We have to get back home. Our parents…"

"If your parents were in that town when the portal went off, they're probably dead," the soldier said.

All four of the kids stared at him with open mouths.

"Way to show some sympathy, Rodgers," another soldier said to the first one, then also gestured at the kids. "He's right though. If you don't want to be as dead as everyone else in your town, you better follow us."

With nothing else to do or say, Murky, Laura, Jesse, and Henderson went with the soldiers out into the field.

CHAPTER TWO

Now that any pretense of hiding seemed to be over, the soldiers were openly walking around as the kids were directed to the temporary base that had been set up in the field. Just because they weren't hiding though, didn't mean they weren't all visibly on edge. Murky could see that every single one of them was nervous, and the mood wasn't helped by the steady thrumming that could still be felt in the ground.

"Where are you taking us?" Laura asked.

"Out of the way," the lead soldier said. "You kids really have no idea what you lucked out of experiencing."

"Could someone please explain what's going on at least?" Jesse asked.

"That's classified," the soldier responded.

There were four or five tents that had been erected here, although from what Murky could tell from the broken bits of walkie-talkie chatter they could hear, this wasn't the only camp that had been set up. It seemed there were stations like this set up all around the town, although no one would tell them why. The soldier led them to one tent that looked like it was full of some kind of supplies and then told them to get inside. The four of them did as they were told for now, and as the soldier left, Murky could hear him ordering two more soldiers to stand guard on them.

"What the hell is going on?" Jesse asked. "This can't be real."

"Laura, did that guy really say everyone in town is dead?" Murky asked.

"I'm sure he was lying to us," Laura said, although she didn't sound like she was sure she believed it.

"Did he say something about a portal?" Henderson asked. "What was he talking about?"

"And what was that light and noise?" Jesse asked.

"I don't know!" Laura said, her normally calm voice rising, giving hint to hidden hysteria underneath. "I don't know the answer to any of this."

Jesse glanced around the tent, then dropped his voice to a whisper. "I bet you we could get out of here pretty easy. It doesn't look like they set this place up with the idea of keeping anyone in it."

"Sure, but where would we go?" Henderson asked. "We're still in a camp surrounded by soldiers who could blow our heads off."

"They wouldn't really do that," Murky said. "Would they?"

Laura shrugged. Before they could discuss any of this any further, they heard raised voices from outside the front tent flap.

"Damn it, I'm not here to look after a bunch of kids."

"Well, you don't seem to be here for any reason, if you ask me."

"What was that? What did you just say?"

"Nothing, ma'am."

"Yeah, right. I bet."

The flap got pulled aside and a woman with red hair and a black suit walked in. She let the flap close behind her, not even bothering to hold it for the soldier that had escorted her here. It didn't sound like the soldier was that interested in them anymore anyway.

She sighed when she saw the four of them. "This whole thing just keeps getting more complicated the worse it becomes."

All four of them started talking at once, most of them asking the same questions about what was going on, what was happening in the town, was everyone really dead...

"All right, hold on, stop," the woman said as she held up her hands. "One at a time, and I honestly can't guarantee that I can answer any of your questions anyway."

"What was that flash of light?" Laura asked.

"That's classified."

"Why is the military here?" Jesse asked.

"That's classified."

"When are you going to let us go?" Henderson asked.

"Probably also classified."

"Then what the hell is even not classified?" Henderson asked. "If I ask you if Redline Flight Cranks are included on the Skyway T/A BMX, are you going to say that's classified, too?"

"I... I don't have any clue what that means, so I couldn't tell you if it's classified or not."

Murky had to hold back tears as she spoke.

"Are Mom and Dad really dead?"

The woman cussed softly to herself. "Jesus, is that really what they told you?" She paused, obviously giving careful thought to her answer. "No, your parents aren't dead. Probably. Not yet, at least."

"What do you mean, not yet?" Laura asked.

The woman paced around a couple of times before she appeared to come to a decision. "Okay, look. I don't care what's classified or not. You four obviously have a right to at least have a clue about what's going on."

"Who even are you?" Henderson asked.

"For now you can call me Agent Larson."

"Agent for what?" Jesse asked. "The FBI?"

Agent Larson smiled a little at that. "We'll just say that for now. I'd give you the real answer, but…"

All four of the kids spoke at once. "It's classified."

"Now you're starting to get it. As for what's going on, well, most people probably wouldn't be surprised to know that the government has been doing a lot of secret things as part of the Cold War. We've got to try to stay ahead of the Russians."

"So the Russians did this?" Murky asked.

Larson shook her head. "This wasn't the Russians. This… this was our fault. There was a secret project some way away from here. Discoveries were made, and they were being studied in a hope that we could weaponize them. In the latest attempt to study the phenomena, a miscalculation was made. Something that was supposed to happen in the lab went elsewhere, and… well…"

"Please don't say 'it's classified,' again," Henderson said.

"It is, but… honestly, I don't care anymore. I've been assigned to the project as a liaison, but no one has been listening to me when I said things were getting out of control. It's my military counterparts who are responsible for blowing the lid off this thing. The responsibility for people knowing is no longer on me."

She looked around at a few of the supply crates that had been haphazardly stacked in the tent and went to sit down on one of them. "It's called Project Subterranea. It's an offshoot of a previous project that investigated the possibility of alternate realities and other dimensions. Subterranea refers to a specific dimension that was discovered. We don't know if it's from Earth in another time period, or a different planet altogether, or a parallel world or universe. All we know is that the portals we've discovered open onto some kind of underground world, a world full of things that we have only begun to imagine."

Jesse looked at her with unabashed wonder. "Really? That doesn't sound like a bad thing at all. That sounds awesome!"

"It was, except then something on the other side realized we were poking holes into their world."

"What kind of something?" Laura asked.

"Ant-like creatures. Giant ones, the size of humans, except with eight legs instead of six. They walk on the back four and use the front four like arms."

"Really?" Murky said with undisguised interest.

"That's even more awesome!" Jesse said.

"I don't know what's crazier," Larson said. "That I'm just blabbing away government secrets to a bunch of kids, or that you're believing all of this without calling me a liar."

"I'll call you a liar if you want," Henderson

said. "I can call you a lot worse things than that, too."

"Not helping, Henderson," Laura said.

"The first time we opened the portal and found them on the other side, they swarmed out and kidnapped a large number of our personnel as well as our scientists. I tried to convince everyone that it was too dangerous to open the portal again, but the general in charge of the military side of the project was convinced we could get some of these ants and, I don't know, breed them as super-soldiers or something. He was always pretty nutty. So they programmed the machinery to open again, this time with plenty of soldiers on the other side to capture some. It was not as easy as the general expected. Some other giant creature came out of the hole first and wiped out most of his forces before the ants invaded again. This time, the machinery used to open and close the portal was damaged. We suspected the portal was going to open again by itself, but not in the lab any longer."

"So it just opened in the middle of Kettle Hollow?" Laura asked.

"That was the flash and rumble you felt. The portal to that underground world is right in the center of your town. No one has gone into town yet, but surveillance suggests it's just like at the lab. The ant things poured out of it and grabbed everyone, then pulled them back in. We have no way of telling yet if anyone in the town escaped them. Except for you four, that is."

"Why are you still surrounding the town then, if it's over?" Laura asked.

"In the lab, the portal would only stay open for so long. There were fail-safes in place to close it after a maximum of fifteen minutes. But surveillance shows that it's not closing. There's no way to shut it down, and no way to be certain more things, things much worse than giant ants, might not come out."

"What happens to the people after the ants take them?" Murky asked.

"We have no idea. We've never sent anyone in after them. All we know is that the underground tunnels go on for a long way, and that something down there is providing light so that it's not completely dark."

"And you're not going to send anyone in after them now?" Jesse asked.

"The general in charge of the military side of

the operation has forbidden it. Their goal is to contain anything trying to come out, and to find a way to close the portal permanently. They've decided that the townsfolk are an unfortunate but necessary loss."

"Necessary?" Laura asked incredulously. "Those are our family and friends!"

"I'm sorry," Agent Larson said. "I truly am. But there's nothing more I can do."

They were all quiet for a moment before Henderson said, "We could do it."

"Excuse me?"

"You could let us go," Laura said. "We could be the ones to go into the center of town and go in looking for them."

"You've got to be joking," Agent Larson said.

"What harm could it do?" Laura asked.

"Wha… what harm? Kid, this is not a game. If any of you go down there, you'll be killed."

"And if we hadn't been out biking by the quarry, we would be down there anyway and still killed," Laura said.

"Yeah, think of the paperwork if you keep us up here," Jesse said. "Also, think of the fact that we actually know what's going on now and we can totally go tell the news."

"No one would believe you," Larson said.

"If we go down there and don't come back, then you don't have to worry about whether or not that's true," Laura said.

Agent Larson appeared to think about this for a few seconds. "Okay, look, here's what I'm thinking. This is nuts, but they won't let me send anyone down that's more capable. Maybe, though, there's a way to help you that might give you a very small chance to actually do this."

She checked the labels on a couple of the crates until she found one marked "Experimental Communications." It was metal and locked shut, but Agent Larson pulled a key out from the pocket of her suit and unlocked it.

"Okay, wait, so you're actually going to let us do this?"

"I'd rather not be responsible for the deaths of four kids, but whatever cover story my agency concocts to hide what happened here tonight, I don't actually trust that they wouldn't make you vanish anyway just to keep it consistent. Being honest here, if I don't let you go try this, then you may very well be on borrowed time anyway."

"This is nuts," Jesse said, but he didn't seem afraid. Murky was the only one of them who seemed frightened of what could happen, but she didn't want to be the weak little one among them.

"Here." Larson pulled out something that looked similar to a walkie-talkie, but it was much larger and heavier. "One of the things we developed for Project Subterranea was a way to communicate that wouldn't be interfered with by all the stone in the way. It's experimental and expensive, but maybe if you take this, I'll still be able to communicate with you while you're down there. I don't know how much advice I'll be able to give you, but at least you won't be doing this completely blind."

Laura took the device and put it in her backpack. It was a tight fit with all the homework she already had in there and the device's antenna poked out through the open zipper, but she would be able to carry it that way.

"Okay, but how do we get out of here and back to town?" Henderson asked. "Are you just going to walk us in like that's a totally normal thing to do?"

"I'm going to walk out the front flap," Agent Larson said. "Wait exactly two minutes, then go to the back of the tent and lift up the canvas to get under it. There're guards there now, but I'll make sure there aren't when you leave. The soldiers grabbed your bikes, so you should find them back there, too. There's a dirt road just to the east of here. The entrance is blocked off from the highway, so the military isn't wasting any man power to guard it."

"That will take us most of the way back in to town," Laura said.

"Once you're in town, you won't be able to dilly-dally," Agent Larson said. "We may be keeping our distance, but there's cameras pointed at it from every direction. The general will probably see you enter and try to stop you, so you'll have to get to the portal and go down as quickly as you can."

"Won't you get in trouble once they find out we escaped?" Murky asked.

"I honestly don't care anymore," Larson said. "After tonight, I'm done with all of this. They put an entire town of innocent people at risk. One way or the other, it's time for me to take an early retirement."

She went back to the front flap but gave them one last look before she left.

"Good luck, but I've got to be honest: I don't think I'm going to see you four ever again."

Then she left.

CHAPTER THREE

After counting to exactly one-hundred and twenty Mississippi, the kids did as they had been instructed and snuck out under the back canvas of the tent. Agent Larson was true to her word in that there was no one waiting there, but their bikes were piled unceremoniously to one side where they could easily get them. Quietly, they all grabbed their bikes and went in the direction Larson had indicated. There seemed to be angry shouting from elsewhere in the camp, but none of them dared see what it was about. Agent Larson was probably providing them with a distraction.

They took their bikes quickly down the path, none of them daring to speak at all until they were at the backyard of one of the houses at the edge of town. Henderson was the first to speak up. "Anyone else expecting to wake up any time now?"

"I don't know," Murky said. "It doesn't seem

that weird to me."

"The military locking down our town and a portal to another dimension full of ant people doesn't seem weird to you?" Laura asked.

"Of course it's weird," Murky said. "Stuff like this usually doesn't happen in Kettle Hollow."

"Murky, stuff like this doesn't usually happen anywhere," Laura responded.

Murky shrugged. "I don't know. I bet it does all the time and just no one talks about it."

It was eerie passing by the various houses on the way to the center of town. Kettle Hollow was small enough that they knew almost every person by name, as well as who should be in which houses doing what at this time of the evening. Old Mrs. Harmsen should have been in her house with the television blaring as she watched *The Cosby Show* or *Highway to Heaven*. Annette Schuler should have been practicing her trumpet. Mr. Turnbull should have been closing up the pharmacy and harassing any kids who were dawdling by the magazine rack. But everything was dark and quiet except for the continued low rumble that emanated from the town's center.

"Maybe we should check some of the houses,"

Laura said. "Just in case anyone is still here."

"What good would it do if they are?" Henderson asked.

"They might be able to come with us and help get everyone else back."

"If we found another kid, then maybe," Henderson said. "But if we found an adult, all they would try to do is stop us."

Laura looked like she wanted to argue, but Murky could tell that she couldn't convince herself that he was wrong.

"It would take too long to look anyway," Jesse said. "Kettle Hollow may be small, but you heard Agent Larson. As soon as the military guys realize we're poking around where they don't want us to, they're going to come for us. We need to get to that portal before they can stop us."

The buzzing sound grew deeper the closer they got to the center of town, and occasional flashes of electricity arced up in the air from the main intersection. It seemed pretty obvious to all of them where the portal was. What surprised them though, was the sheer size of it. When Murky had heard the word "portal," she'd confused it with a "port hole" and imagined it to be something small, like a little round window that they would barely be able to fit through. Instead what they found was a massive hole in the ground nearly thirty feet in diameter. It could have looked like a semi-natural phenomenon, a sink hole that might have collapsed open in the middle of the intersection, except for the edges of the portal, which had a static blue color and hurt Murky's eyes to look at it. The edges of the hole were rotating fast in a clockwise fashion, like dyed water going down a drain, except the border was only half a foot wide before showing the hole beyond.

"It looks like a swirly," Jesse muttered.

"A what?" Murky asked.

"A swirly," Henderson said. "It's when someone dunks his head in a toilet and flushes it."

"Um, I don't think the swirly itself looks like this, just the water when it flushes," Laura said.

"Says someone who's never had her head stuck in the middle of one," Jesse muttered.

Beyond the edge of the portal, right where the town's lone stoplights should have been, there was a ragged edge of rock followed by a steep drop off into darkness below. Along the edges there were a series of stairs carved into the stone. The stairs didn't look like they had been there until recently, as they were rough and looked like they'd been carved hastily, but also they seemed to be at very strange angles and sizes, like they had not at all been designed for humans to walk on them. The stairs twisted and turned over various outcroppings as they went deeper down into the dark, but instead of being pitch black, the deepest depths of the hole had a haunting dark green glow.

"I wonder what's causing that," Laura said.

"Maybe the rocks have some kind of chemical reaction," Jesse said. "Or maybe there's something down there that's bioluminescent."

"I have absolutely no idea what that means," Henderson said.

"Maybe we don't have to do this after all," Murky said. "Maybe we can go back and get them to change their minds."

Jesse turned to frown at her. "Murky, have you ever known an adult to change their mind when they're wrong?"

Murky shrugged. He had a point.

They all hesitated at the edge, none of them wanting to be the first to step over the strange border and begin the climb down those stone steps.

"Are we sure this is safe?" Murky asked.

"No," Henderson said. "In fact, I'm pretty sure this is all the exact opposite of safe."

"Hey, does anyone else hear that?" Laura asked.

"Yeah, it's pretty hard *not* to hear it," Jesse said. "That buzzing hum thing is rattling my teeth."

"Not that," Laura said. "I thought I heard…"

She didn't need to finish that thought, because now they could all hear the clear sounds of engines as multiple vehicles drove in their direction. Since there was little chance of it being someone driving through town at this point, none of them needed to point out that it was probably trucks and Jeeps full of military personnel, all of them on their way to stop the four kids from interfering, even if there wasn't exactly much to interfere with at this exact moment.

"I think that means time's up," Laura said. "Last chance for anyone to turn back. You could probably hide in one of the buildings and not be noticed. Murky?"

"I don't want to go down there," Murky said, "but I don't want to go back, either. So I'm going with you."

"Jesse?"

"Um, yeah. Sure. I'm going. It'll be fun, right?" Jesse didn't sound at all convinced, but he also didn't seem to want to turn back.

"Henderson?"

"Hell yeah I'm heading down there. Let's stomp some ant people butts. And you, Laura?"

"My parents are down there," she said simply. "Let's go."

When no one else made the move to be the first to step into the portal, Laura gingerly put a foot over the strange swirling blue energy and onto the first step. Murky had no idea what would happen if any of them stuck their feet or hands in the energy itself, but she didn't want to find out. As Laura started down the steep stairs, Murky followed her, with Jesse behind her and Henderson in the rear. They were all just down below the edge of the rock when the vehicles came to a stop nearby and multiple voices began shouting at them to stop.

"No more time," Henderson said. "Everyone, move!"

They did the closest thing they could to running down the spiraling stairs, but the sizes of the steps themselves made running awkward. Also, Murky found she couldn't make herself go too fast for fear that she might lose her balance and go tumbling down into the abyss. Once they were about twenty feet down, she risked looking over the edge, then immediately wished she hadn't. She thought she could see a floor slanting off into the green glow somewhere below them, but it certainly wasn't near. If any of them slipped and fell over the side, they wouldn't survive the fall, at least not from here.

There were more shouts from above them, and Murky looked up to see several soldiers peering over the ledge, their guns pointed down at the four kids.

They wouldn't, Murky thought. As soon as she thought it, several bullets flew through the air and chipped the strange rock outcroppings around them.

"They're actually shooting!" Jesse yelled. "What the hell?"

"You idiots, stop shooting!" someone else called from up top. Murky thought it might be Agent Larson; already the cavern around them was creating a strange echo effect that made it difficult to be certain.

"But we can't let them go down there!" someone yelled back. An argument began, but

Murky didn't hear much of it. They weren't so far down yet that the soldiers couldn't give chase, but it was obvious that none of them wanted to cross the swirling blue line of the portal if they didn't have to. Now that the military wasn't shooting at them, they seemed to be in the clear to continue.

Just as she thought that, Murky heard a shout of surprise from behind her. She turned to see that Henderson must have slipped and fallen on a step, because he was on his stomach with one leg and one arm dangling out into the drop. Jesse stopped to grab him, and both Murky and Laura went back up a few steps to help. The stairs under Henderson looked like they might be ready to crumble, but thankfully none of them were particularly heavy and they were able to pull him from the edge before he could be put in too much danger. Henderson looked shaken, but he didn't stop to say anything. He just gestured for them to go on ahead, and they did so with as much haste as they could without actually putting themselves in danger again.

Within a couple of minutes, they reached the bottom. When Murky looked up, she could no longer see anyone else looking down at them from the top of the shaft.

They had made it, but they were now also alone.

CHAPTER FOUR

At first there seemed to be two separate tunnels they could go down at the base of the stairs, but a quick inspection of one showed that it led to a dead end except for a hole in the ceiling snaking off in a general up direction. That could have been the direction they truly needed to go, for all they knew, but since they didn't have any way to climb up it, they had no other choice but to go down the other direction, a wide hall roughly the width of Kettle Hollow's Main Street.

It was here that they finally got a good look at what was causing the cave system's eerie green glow. There was some kind of fungus or lichen growing on almost every available inch of the walls and ceiling, and it gave off varying degrees of faint light like dying fireflies. The floor probably would have been covered with it as well if it weren't for the fact that there seemed to be regular foot traffic through here, resulting in a smooth path down the middle of the cave floor with dead and trampled fungus along the sides.

They went down this direction for a little way in silence before Laura stopped them. "Okay, we really need to come up with some kind of game plan here. We can't just go wandering around these tunnels with no idea what we're doing."

"Does anybody have anything in their backpacks that could help us?" Jesse asked.

"I never have the slightest clue what I've left in my backpack," Henderson said.

"I think all I've got is homework," Laura said. "That, and that communicator Agent Larson gave us."

Nevertheless, she shouldered off her backpack and unzipped it. They all stooped down on the ground as they emptied the contents to get a better idea of what they had to work with.

"Yeah. Just pens, pencils, a notebook, and my social studies book," Laura said. "What about you, Jesse? What do you have?"

"A Trapper Keeper, a gum wrapper, and my math book. Henderson?"

"Um, just my gym shirt." Henderson pulled it

out and tossed it on the ground with the rest of the increasingly useless pile of items.

"Ew, gross!" Jesse said. "That thing smells totally disgusting. Why is it in your backpack instead of your gym locker?"

"My gym teacher said it was the worst smelling thing in the locker, so he made me take it home to wash it."

Laura gingerly picked it up and handed it back to him, then started putting her own things back in her pack. "What about you, Murky? Knowing the way you squirrel away things, you've got to have something in there that isn't homework."

Murky reached into her backpack and pulled out the only thing inside that seemed like it could possibly be useful. "I've got a bag of marshmallows," she said.

Laura gave her a look like she thought Murky was crazy while Henderson threw up his hands in disgust. "Great. Marshmallows. I'm sure that will come in *real* handy against the army of alien ant creatures," he said.

"Why do you even have those?" Jesse asked her.

Murky shrugged. "Just in case I need

something to roast over a campfire."

"Why would you expect to just randomly run into campfires?" Henderson asked.

She shrugged again. "You never know."

"Okay, so what if we've got nothing useful," Jesse said. "We can still do this, right?" He didn't sound like he believed it. Rather, it sounded like he wanted someone else to convince him, but no one else responded.

"We at least have this," Laura said, hefting up the heavy communicator device. "It's not going to be fun to lug it around, though."

"Man, that agent lady probably should have given us flashlights instead," Henderson said.

"She shouldn't have had to give us anything," Jesse said. "We're just kids. It shouldn't be us that are doing this. It should have been all the people up top with huge guns."

"You sure weren't acting like you didn't want to do this while we were still in the tent," Henderson said.

"Yeah, well that was before I saw all the empty houses and the creepy hole and climbed down it to hang out with who knows what," Jesse said.

"Yeah? Well, what did you expect?"

Henderson asked. "The adults to actually be useful? When have you known adults to treat kids like anything other than crap?"

"Our parents treat us good," Murky said softly.

"Yeah, well your parents are the exception," Henderson said. "My dad… he's…" He stopped for a long time before continuing. Somehow, the other three all knew not to speak up yet. "I guess he tries. Sort of. What if he's dead? What if he's gone now too and I'm alone?"

There was a long pause as the other three tried to think of something to say. "I've met your dad," Jesse finally said. "He wouldn't give up without punching a few ant people on the way down. And my mom would bash them over the head with a frying pan. They'll be fine, as long as we can get to them."

"We can do this, right?" Laura asked. Everyone stared at her, but she wouldn't look back at them. Instead she stared up at the green glowing ceiling as though it held all the answers if only she stared at it hard enough. Finally, when she did look at them, she had a look in her eye that Murky knew well. That was the look her big sister got when she felt too stubborn to let other people tell her what to do.

It wasn't a look she pulled out often, but Murky had seen it enough times that she both respected and feared it. "We can do this. We *will* do this."

As they finished putting all their things back in their backpacks, no one dared question her. Still, even with her sister's determination, Murky wasn't so sure they were going to be going back up those stairs into Kettle Hollow ever again.

CHAPTER FIVE

Murky found herself tiring of all the walking pretty quickly. All four of them were in good shape for their age, but considering they had just run down a set of rock stairs deep into some underground dimension, and it was also getting to be past her normal bedtime, it made sense that she was going to be low on energy. She reached around to her backpack and pulled out a few marshmallows, eating one and then offering the rest to the others. They all accepted, even Henderson after the way he had mocked her for having them. Murky felt pretty good about that.

Their first major obstacle occurred after about fifteen minutes. The tunnel had expanded into something roughly large enough for a semi to drive through and then forked into two different directions. They all stopped and considered the branching paths, but it was obvious to Murky that they were all waiting to see what Laura would say they should do.

"I don't have the slightest clue which way we should go," Laura finally said.

"Maybe now would be a good time to take out that communicator phone thing," Jesse said. "Agent Larson has got to know more about this place than we do, right?"

"She didn't sound like she knew that much when we were talking to her earlier," Henderson said.

"Still, it can't hurt to try," Laura said. She unshouldered her backpack and pulled out the communicator. "I'm not even sure how to turn this stupid thing on." They fiddled with it for nearly a minute before they got it to turn on and make some sort of scratching hiss noise. The sound was disturbingly loud in the tunnel. Murky hoped there was nothing down here with them that could hear it.

"Agent Larson, are you there?" Laura asked into the part of the device that looked like it might have been a microphone or a speaker. She turned to look at the others. "Should I use this the same way people use walkie-talkies? Should I be saying 'over' or '10-4, good buddy,' or something?"

There was a crackle from the device before Larson's tinny voice came through it. "You don't need to do any of that. Just speak into it the way you would a phone."

Henderson snorted. "A portable, wireless phone? Yeah right. When Huffy starts making airplanes, maybe."

"I can hear all of you," Larson said. "This is good. I wasn't completely sure this was going to work. We never had the chance to give these things a proper field test."

"Right, so we're down here," Laura said. "Now what?"

"First of all, are any of you having trouble breathing?"

"Wait," Henderson said. "You sent us down here without even being sure if we could breathe the air?"

"Kid, in case you forgot, I didn't send you anywhere. You were the ones who volunteered. And no, we couldn't be sure that the air would be the same as up here. You're technically in another dimension, don't forget. We were still exploring what the rules even were for it."

"You know, come to think of it, the air down

here does seem different, but not in a bad way," Jesse said. "It's almost easier to breathe, like there's more oxygen."

"That makes a little bit of sense," Agent Larson said. "Bugs shouldn't be able to grow as large as those ants without higher oxygen levels. The only question is where the oxygen would be coming from."

"Maybe it's from the glowing fungus all over the walls," Laura said.

"Could be. I'd ask you to get samples of it to study if it weren't a matter of... wait. Something's going on outside my tent. Keep the communicator turned on. I'll be right back."

"Wait!" Laura said. "Before you go, we need... Agent Larson? Are you still there?"

There was no answer from the other end.

"Great," Henderson said. "Guess we're just going to sit around like jerks while we wait for her to come back and tell us where to go. Well I could tell *her* where to go..."

Murky noticed a thoughtful look come over Jesse's face. "What is it? What are you thinking?"

"I'm wondering if she already told us the direction to go," Jesse said. "Look closely at these two paths. Notice a difference between them?"

They all looked, but nothing immediately jumped out to Murky. "I don't see anything," Henderson said. "Especially not down that one." He pointed at the one to their left. "It looks like it's less glowy."

"Wait, I bet that's exactly what you're talking about, isn't it?" Laura asked.

"Yeah," Jesse said. "If the ant people need lots of oxygen, and we're assuming the fungus is somehow making it, then wouldn't it be more likely that that's the direction they would have taken everyone?"

"That's making a lot of assumptions," Laura said, then looked at the communicator in her hand. "But it's all we've got for now. Let's start down that way. If Agent Larson comes back on and tells us otherwise, we'll just come back and go the other way."

They started in that direction and quickly decided they were probably going the right way. Whether or not Jesse's logic had been correct, the rock floor here was even smoother than the tunnels they'd been in previously, implying it had been well travelled. They also began to see a number of cracks in the wall forming darkened alcoves where the fungus wasn't growing. Henderson went up to one and stuck his head in.

"Henderson, I'm not so sure that's a good idea," Laura said.

"It doesn't look that dangerous to me," Henderson said. "It's big enough for…"

Before he could finish the sentence, something screeched from the direction of the tunnel they had just come from. They all froze.

"What was that?" Murky asked.

"Whatever it is, I don't like the sound of it," Henderson said. "Everyone, hide in here."

He grabbed Murky by the arm and shoved her into the crack. All four of them could fit in it if needed, but it wouldn't be terribly comfortable. Laura was the farthest away, and as she started running for the alcove, the communicator came out of her hands and clattered to the floor. For a moment she looked like she wanted to go back for it, but somewhere behind them something was causing the glow to darken. She ran in after Henderson, with Jesse close behind her.

"Oh God, what is it?" Jesse asked. "What is…"

Henderson put his hand over Jesse's mouth as

he quietly gestured for Murky and Laura to look out in the direction they'd come. They all instinctively pressed themselves tighter up against the nearest rock wall as a shape became more visible in the distant shadows of the tunnel, accompanied by a series of soft noises that were somehow between hisses and grunts.

"Kids, are you still there?" Agent Larson's voice said through the communicator.

The sound grew louder in response.

"We need that communicator doodad," Laura whispered. "It's the only thing we've got going for us."

"Don't look at me," Henderson said. "I'm not going out there to get it until we're sure that whatever that thing out there has gone away."

"Kids, I don't know if you can still hear me, but if we lose the connection, there's something you need to know."

The thing moving down the corridor to them was much louder now, and it was obvious that whatever it was, it was big enough to take up most of the tunnel.

"The general in charge has decided that if we can't close the portal, he might as well try to close it by blowing the town up," Larson's voice said. "It's going to take a while to get enough ordinance, though. So you have about seven hours. After that…"

They didn't get a chance to hear the rest of what Larson was going to say. They all scrunched up tighter against each other in the alcove as the thing that had been coming after them finally arrived. Whatever it was, it was absolutely enormous, and it must have had multiple legs judging by the relentless sound of clicking against the rocks. It went by too fast for any of them to be sure what it was supposed to be, but Murky thought she saw, at the front of the thing, two giant oversized mandibles that took up a significant portion of its entire head. The creature, whatever it was, gave some kind of screeching roar as it passed, but even with as fast as it was going, it took quite a few seconds before it was no longer blocking the entrance to their hidey hole. It was like some kind of organic freight train rushing by them. But even through the noise, Murky was sure she heard the crunching of metal and plastic.

Even after the enormous creature was past their alcove, none of them dared come out until the sounds of its movements were nothing more but distant echoes sounding throughout the caverns. Only once they were sure it wasn't coming back did any of them risk venturing back into the main tunnel.

"Okay, would someone like to tell me what the hell that was?" Henderson asked.

"It was big," Murky said.

"No kidding, Sherlock," Jesse said. "I didn't get a look at it, but it almost might have been some kind of insect."

"That's one huge insect," Laura said.

"We already know we're supposed to be seeing giant bugs down here, but I don't think that was one of the ant people Agent Larson was talking about," Jesse said. "That had to be something else."

"Yeah? Well let's hope it's a something else we don't see again," Henderson said. He went over to the point on the ground where they had dropped the communicator and kicked at the remains. It was shattered beyond all recognition. Whatever that thing had been, it had been big and heavy enough to completely obliterate their only connection back to the world above. "So much for that doohickey."

"Did anyone else hear what Agent Larson said

before that thing came through?" Murky asked. "It sounded like she was saying something about explosions."

"Yeah, I think she did," Laura said. "She said we've got seven hours before the military blows up Kettle Hollow. Maybe less."

"How would they even explain that?" Henderson asked. "An entire town going kaboom would make people pay attention, wouldn't it?"

"They could make up any story, like a gas leak or something," Jesse said. "It would be far-fetched, but still easier to believe than the truth."

"So we don't have any more time to worry about what else might be in these tunnels," Laura said. "We need to get moving."

"Shouldn't be too bad," Henderson said as they all started walking down the tunnel again. "I can't imagine that there's going to be anything crazier than what we've already seen."

It didn't take long at all before he was proven wrong.

CHAPTER SIX

On several occasions they came across more branching paths. There was no way at all they could be certain, but they continued to follow the logic that the presence of the glowing fungus, beyond just making it easier for them to not stumble around blindly, suggested the presence of other life as well. They ended up being right, but they weren't prepared for exactly what kind of life they were about to encounter.

They could tell they were approaching some kind of open cavern by the way the echoes of their voices changed, but none of them were ready to find an open space large enough to hold a small underground city. The tunnel opened out onto a high ledge overlooking the cavern, giving them a perfect view of the creatures grazing in the humongous space below.

The cavern was full of dinosaurs.

"That is so rad!" Jesse whispered. "Real, actual breathing dinosaurs!"

While Murky may have been obsessed with animals, she had never read up much on dinosaurs, so she was at a loss to give an exact name to any of the creatures roaming around down there in the cavern. She still recognized plenty of them though, names or not. Nearest to their hiding place she could see a small group of the kind with ridges and horns around their heads, while much further out she thought she could see the huge scary kind with big teeth as it ran after some kind of prey.

"Maybe we could go down there and pet one of them?" Murky asked.

"Murky, I'm sorry, but we've got a lot more important things to do right now than try to pet giant lizards," Laura said. She tapped her wrist, even though she had left her colorful Swatch watch at home because she'd been afraid of wrecking it while biking. "Tick, tick, tick."

Murky stuck her lip out in a pout, but she wasn't going to argue with her big sister.

"We might still have to go down there anyway," Henderson said. "I don't see any other way to go, do you?"

They all looked around themselves, but they could tell right away that he was right. To one side there was a well-worn path that sloped down from their cliff and onto the main floor of the dinosaurs' cavern. Down on the cavern floor there seemed to be a couple of different tunnels that they might choose to go through, but up here there was no way to go except the way they had come.

"As cool as it would be to get close to one," Laura said, "I think we need to find a path through down there that keeps us as far away from them as possible."

"Yeah, even the ones that wouldn't eat us could probably still stomp on us," Henderson said.

"We can't even go and touch just one of them?" Murky asked. "Not even one of the little ones?"

"Murky, don't even think about it," Laura said. "We don't have the time to go rescuing one of us if that person's about to get trampled."

Murky pouted at her but nodded. "Fine. Be a spoil sport."

They all went down the slope as quietly as possible, partly out of awe for their situation and partly for fear of triggering some kind of stampede from the creatures three and four times their size. The closer they got though, the more it seemed that the prehistoric creatures were completely unimpressed by the four of them. Several of them looked directly at the four kids descending the slope into their domain and then went right back to whatever important dino business they felt they needed to do. A lot of them, at least the ones that didn't seem to be meat eaters, were munching away at the glowing fungus, as well as a large number of other mushroom-like things, some of which by themselves were six or seven feet high. Every once in a while they thought they could hear one of the more carnivorous types roar in the distance, but there were enough dinosaurs here that the plant-eaters didn't actually seem to mind that a few of them might end up as snacks.

"This is so crazy," Laura said once they were on the cavern floor. "How is this even possible?"

"We're in an underground dimension trying to find the ant people that kidnapped our town," Henderson said. "How is any of this possible?"

"But this is different than giant insect species that seem to have evolved differently," Jesse said. "These are dinosaurs from millions of years ago that look more or less like they would have in our dimension back then. How did they get here? Why haven't they changed with time to be something completely different that suits the environment? These are questions we need to ask."

"We don't need to ask anything science-y at all, nerd," Henderson said. "We just need to get through it and out. We'll let Larson and her eggheads try to figure out the why when we get out. *If* we get out."

"Oh come on, man," Jesse said. "You don't wonder at all why there are *dinosaurs* in an underground sub-dimension?"

"Nope," Henderson said.

"You're no fun," Jesse responded.

Despite the earlier admonition from her older sister that they couldn't dawdle, Murky found herself frequently stopping to stare at the majestic creatures milling around in the cavern, and the other three did very little to keep her on track. Indeed, they often stopped right alongside her to stare in awe. Jesse would occasionally chime in with their names, and Murky did her best to remember each and every one – triceratops, brachiosaurus, tyrannosaurus rex, iguanodon, ankylosaurus, dimetrodon, pterodactyl. The words made little sense to her, but she didn't need them to. She would probably never see animals like this ever again, and she wanted to appreciate every single moment she had with them. She even wondered if she would still have the same sense of wonder for things like bats and raccoons ever again.

"Watching them makes me feel so small," Laura said in a hushed tone.

"I always feel small," Murky said.

"I mean, not like physically," Laura said. "I mean in the grand scheme of things. Here's a giant cave full of creatures that were supposed to be dead millions of years ago. And to get to them, we had to go through a glowing blue portal to another dimension. Doesn't that make anyone else feel insignificant?"

"You're only insignificant if you let yourself be insignificant," Henderson said. "And I'm anything but insignificant." Despite his words, Murky couldn't help but notice that his tone matched Laura's. She didn't think he was as unaffected by all this as he was trying to seem.

"They're really just ignoring us, aren't they?" Jesse said. "They don't care that we're walking among them at all. They've probably never seen anything like us before. They don't seem to have any idea that maybe they should be scared of us, or that maybe we might be food."

"Let's not go and say that until we're away from them," Henderson said. "You might jinx us."

Down on the cavern floor there were a large number of tunnels that could be seen branching among the walls, but most of them would have been too small for any of the dinosaurs to get through. If they needed to, they could run down any one of them to get to safety at any time, but most of them lacked the glowing fungus that they'd been using as their guide.

"I don't know if using the fungus is going to be the best option to figure out where to go here," Henderson said. "There's too many different paths."

"Most of the paths don't have it, though," Jesse said.

"But the number of paths that do have it are more than one," Laura said. "Henderson may be right here. We might need to try a different way to track down the townspeople."

They'd passed the largest portion of the dinosaur herds, but Murky stopped listening to her companions and instead concentrated on the noises of the various creatures. She'd thought she heard something behind them, but when she turned to look, all she saw was a number of shadowy caves.

And, she realized, something moving around in those shadows. It was something much smaller than most of the things they'd seen down here so far, but she was pretty certain that, whatever it was, it wasn't human.

"Hey guys?" she said. "I think something's following us."

Henderson looked doubtful about that, but Laura immediately took her seriously. "What kind of something?"

"I don't know. But look over there." Murky pointed into a darkened tunnel. "I thought I saw…"

Something in the darkness opened its green, piercing, reptilian eyes. They caught a slight glow from distant fungus, making the eyes appear as though they shined with their own light. Although they still couldn't make out the thing's shape, they definitely heard it hiss as something disconnected from the shadows and ran right toward them.

CHAPTER SEVEN

"Run!" Jesse screamed. They all started running, but it was obvious right away that none of them were sure which direction would be the best one to run to. Murky went one way and Henderson another, while both Laura and Jesse went straight for the largest tunnel opening they could see with a significant amount of the fungus. Henderson recognized right away that they were probably moving in a smarter direction, but Murky wasn't thinking clearly enough to run after them. Instead she ran for the nearest tunnel, one that had a dim glow from fungus but was still much darker than any other path they had gone down yet. Behind her she heard something running, something with sharp claws that clicked harshly against the stone. Whatever had been hiding in the shadows, it had singled her out as the one it really wanted to go after.

"Murky! Wait! Not that way!" Laura called out to her, but Murky's panic took over her and kept her running up until she found herself up against a rock wall with nowhere else to go. She turned around, certain that she was about to see some monster ready to rip her to shreds and eat her, only to find the tunnel empty. She didn't dare move, though. Whatever the thing had been, it was obviously good at hiding in the shadows, and anything at all that she did might give her position away to it.

"Murky? Where are you?" Henderson called from out in the main cavern. After about thirty seconds, she heard several footsteps as her three companions entered the tunnel.

"Murky?" Laura asked, her voice full of genuine concern.

"Are you sure this is the tunnel she went in?" Henderson asked.

"No, I'm not sure, but this was the last direction I saw her running in before I lost track of whatever that was after us," Laura said.

"Maybe that thing got her," Jesse said.

"You shut your damn mouth with that," Laura said in an uncharacteristically harsh tone. "My sister is going to be perfectly fine."

Murky looked very closely around her in the shadows, making sure she was truly alone, before she called out to them. "I'm over here!"

The other three ran down the length of the tunnel to find her cowering in the corner. "Murky! Are you okay?" Laura asked as she hugged her little sister. "Where did that creature go?"

"I don't know," Murky said. "I thought it was right behind me. But then when I got in here…"

A low growl sounded from back in the direction of the tunnel opening. They all turned to it and saw a shape silhouetted against the brighter glow from other tunnels.

"Uh, crap," Jesse said. "I think it set up a trap for us. And we all just walked into it."

They all huddled against the wall next to Murky as the thing took several slow steps closer to them. It was about six or seven feet tall, and from the front it appeared to be vaguely lizard-like, or maybe more like a huge scary bird. It had a long, thick tail whipping back and forth behind it that seemed to be for balancing, and the closer it got, the more Murky thought it might be some kind of small version of the tyrannosaurus rex that they had seen roaming around out in the main cavern.

"What is it?" Murky asked quietly. "Is it a dinosaur?"

"It's too small to be a dinosaur," Henderson said. "Dinosaurs are huge."

"Nuh-uh," Jesse said. "There were plenty of them that were smaller."

"The smaller ones were less dangerous, right?" Laura asked.

"Um, again, that's not exactly true." There was a noticeable stutter in Jesse's voice as he shook with fear.

The closer the creature got, the more they could see of it. It was dark and rough skinned, there were a few parts here and there that looked like they might have had strange feather-like protrusions on them. On its feet and its short arms it had very large, wicked-looking claws, and its mouth was full of razor-sharp teeth. Strangely enough, despite these intimidating features, Murky found herself becoming less and less afraid the closer it got to them. If it wanted to attack them it could have already. Its mannerisms didn't seem predatory at all at the moment, either. If anything, it looked like it was more curious about them than anything else.

"Hello," Murky said as pleasantly as she could

manage. The dinosaur stopped a few feet away from them and made a couple of strange little chirping noises.

"Murky, what do you think you're…" Laura started to say, but Murky ignored her and took a step toward the creature. When it didn't react negatively to the motion, she took off her backpack, unzipped it, and pulled out the bag of marshmallows. Murky tore open a hole in the bag and held one out.

"Would you like a marshmallow?" Murky asked.

The dinosaur cocked its head at the offered treat.

"Go on," Murky said. "It's tasty. I promise."

"Um, Murky?" Henderson said. "Maybe you shouldn't be using the word 'tasty' at it while it's staring at us like that."

The dinosaur took a couple of tentative steps forward, sniffing the air. Murky wasn't sure if the marshmallow smelled like anything at all to it, but it hadn't ripped her arm off yet, so maybe that was a good sign.

"Maybe it's a nice dinosaur," Murky said. "Like those ones down there with long necks eating the mushrooms."

"No, I don't think it is," Jesse said. "That looks like some kind of version of a velociraptor."

"Never heard of it," Henderson said.

"Let's just say there's nothing in any of my books about them eating marshmallows."

Yet the velociraptor really did seem intrigued by the puffy white treat in her hand. Not wanting to get too close, Murky tossed it the remaining foot in the dinosaur's direction. It deftly snapped the marshmallow out of the air and chewed exactly twice before swallowing it down. It cocked its head as though considering what it had just tasted, then made a sound that Murky could only interpret as "Can I have another?"

"Yeah, of course you can!" Murky said as she pulled out the next marshmallow.

"Uh, Murky? Who are you talking to?" Henderson asked.

"Never mind her when she does that," Laura said. "She goes and thinks she knows what animals are thinking, then forgets that other people would find it weird when she replies. It's something you get used to."

"You're not so bad," Murky said as she offered it the marshmallow. This time she didn't throw it, instead growing bold and getting closer to the velociraptor. It could have easily chomped down on her and severed her hand, but instead it almost daintily took the marshmallow from her fingers and chewed. "Hey Laura, I think I made a friend. What should I call him?"

"How do you even know it's a him?" Henderson asked.

"I don't, but I'm sure he would tell me if I was wrong."

By the time she was finished giving him everything that had been in the marshmallow bag, she had completely lost all fear of the creature. Even though Laura made nervous noises behind her, Murky went right up to the velociraptor and tried to pet its head. It didn't seem especially pleased at the touch, but neither did it try to shy away or attack her.

"I'm going to call him Chicago," Murky said.

"What?" Jesse asked. "Why would you call him that?"

"Because that's his name. I decided so just now."

"Murky, you can't just name a dinosaur after a city," Henderson said.

"Why not?"

"I mean, just think about it. Who would call a dinosaur Minneapolis? San Francisco? Denver?"

"It doesn't matter what she wants to name him," Laura said. "He doesn't get a name because we're getting away from him as quickly as we can."

"What? Why?" Murky asked. "Can't we take him with us?"

Henderson shook his head. "Murky, we can't just walk around with a valet ratchet."

"Um, I think you mean velociraptor," Jesse said.

Henderson shrugged. "Whatever. It's still something that will try to eat us as soon as it's finished digesting those marshmallows."

"He's right, Murky," Laura said. "Good job on stopping him from attacking us, but we have to get out of here now. He could turn on us at any moment, and we still need to figure out what direction we're even going."

Murky perked up. "Maybe Chicago could help us with that!"

"I doubt that," Henderson said.

"Maybe he can follow the missing people the same way a dog would. Maybe we can have him sniff something one of them touched and then we can follow him to them!"

"One, I don't think dinosaurs work like that," Henderson said. "Two, we don't have anything that could be used for that."

"How do you know a dinosaur doesn't work like that?" Murky asked. "Have you ever met one before?"

"Um, no."

"Then shut up! And maybe he doesn't need something that was owned or touched by one of the others. Maybe he can just follow them by smelling us. I mean, he's probably never seen humans before. We've got to smell strange and easy to track to him."

"I'm not sure that's how logic works," Jesse said.

"Look, let's just get moving," Laura said. "We'll find the tunnel that seems to have the brightest fungus and keep going with the same thinking we were before."

Laura, Jesse, and Henderson carefully skirted around the dinosaur and went back out into the main cavern. Murky pouted but followed them, sure that Chicago would lose interest and run away if she

wasn't continually giving him attention.
He didn't.

CHAPTER EIGHT

"Please tell me he's stopped," Henderson dramatically whispered to Laura. Laura, however, used her normal voice when replying.

"Nope. We've still got a walking razor blade following us like a lost puppy."

"Maybe we can make him stop," Henderson said. "Like, I don't know, whack him on the nose with a rolled-up newspaper."

"A, we don't have any newspaper," Laura said. "And B, if you want to be the one who risks bopping a carnivorous dinosaur on the snout, go ahead and be my guest. I'll be sure to see what I can do to reattach your arm afterward."

"Nobody's hitting him!" Murky said. "He's my friend."

Chicago had been following them for the last ten minutes, but he wasn't doing anything at all to make them think he was stalking them in any way.

If anything, he appeared to want to get closer, especially to Murky, but seemed afraid of what the others might do. Murky was amused by that, a dinosaur that could rip any one of them apart being afraid of a human. A couple of times she had almost been able to coax Chicago to walk right beside them, but he'd backed away and instead followed them from a distance every time.

"Murky, maybe it's not a good idea for you to keep encouraging him like that," Laura said to her.

"Why not?" Murky asked. "This is how I would treat any of my other pets."

"Except this isn't a pet. This is a dinosaur. A meat-eating one. You do realize what that means it will try to eat if it gets hungry enough, right?"

"More marshmallows?"

"You already gave him all your marshmallows."

"Maybe we can find more down here somewhere."

Before Laura could respond, Chicago gave a sudden hiss at something up ahead of them.

"Everyone stop," Henderson said. "I think he's seeing something, or smelling something, or whatever."

"How could he even see anything down here?" Laura asked. "The fungus on the walls is barely illuminating anything right now."

"Also, why are we assuming that something he doesn't like would be something we don't like? Maybe there's something else friendly down here that could help us." Jesse kept walking down through the passage, although he didn't do it with that much confidence. More than anything, he still seemed to just be trying to put extra distance between himself and Chicago.

Laura held out her hand in a stopping gesture. "Jesse, I really don't think you should…"

There was a squish as Jesse stepped on something soft and strange. "Ewwww," he said. "What was…"

He was cut off as something thick and heavy whipped up from the cave floor and slammed him in the legs. Jesse screamed as it knocked him over, but he didn't even get a chance to fall all the way to the cave floor. Some kind of vine or tentacle wrapped around his leg and hoisted him up into the air.

"Jesse!" Henderson called out, but he didn't seem to have any idea what to do. None of them did.

They weren't even sure what was happening until a particularly large spot of glowing fungus farther down the wall started to glow brighter. Other tendrils of fungus had been blocking it off, deliberately making it darker to hide a single, ten-foot tall stalk with what looked like an inverted mushroom cap at the top. The top of the cap had some kind of flap on it, immediately making Murky think of a giant mouth. Inside the flap she could see a hard ring of spikes like teeth. At the base of the stalk she could see a number of rubbery tentacles, including the one that had Jesse, protruding from its base like exposed roots.

"It's some kind of killer plant!" Henderson yelled. He jumped up to try to grab Jesse and pull him out of the tentacle's grasp, but the carnivorous mushroom just pulled Jesse higher in the air and out of reach. As he was jerked up, Jesse yelled something that Laura didn't quite hear.

"What did he say?" Laura asked Murky as they both ran toward the stalk and writhing mass of tentacles.

"I think he said it's a fungus, not a plant," Murky said.

"It's really not the time for that, Jesse!"

Henderson called.

"Whatever!" Jesse called back. "Just get me down before this thing, like, eats me or something!"

To Murky's horror, that did in fact seem like what it was intent on doing. From this angle she couldn't see what was in the mushroom cap beyond the weird toothy thorns, but she could guess there would be enough room in there for the mushroom to swallow Jesse whole. And after it was done with him, it could very well do the same to the rest of them.

"We've got to get him down," Henderson said. "Murky, get up on my shoulders and try to reach his hand."

"I don't think that will... ack!" Murky found herself in the air along with Jesse before she could finish her sentence. The rubbery tentacle fungus had wrapped around her waist while she'd been distracted, and now that she was hefted up, she could clearly see the inside of the mushroom's maw. Down inside the long stalk of the mushroom were more of those tooth-like protrusions, most of them pointing down to keep anything that went in from coming back out. At the bottom there seemed to be some kind of shimmering liquid. Murky thought she'd heard something about how certain plants would trap bugs in them and then digest them in some kind of acid deep inside. She had a feeling that if the tentacles dropped the two of them in there, neither of them would be coming back out.

"Help!" Murky screamed. She wasn't really expecting anyone to be able to do anything, but at the sound of her distressed voice, Chicago hissed.

The dinosaur had been hanging back as the mushroom attacked Jesse, but now that it had Murky, he rushed forward. The tentacles whipped up in the air to grab him and the others, but Henderson and Laura jumped out of the way while Chicago went straight for them, slashing at the vine-like appendages with his sharp claws. The mushroom didn't seem to feel any pain at this, but it was definitely distracted, if distraction was even something it could feel. It dropped Jesse, who landed in a bundle of root-like appendages sticking out of the stem's bottom and bounced off their rubbery outsides. Murky, however, stayed firmly in its grasp, and the tentacle pulled her closer to the waiting maw.

This has to be fine, right? she thought. *There's no way this is actually going to happen.* She continued to think that to herself until she was dangling directly over the opening. At the last second, right as the vine-like appendage let her go, she tried to swing all the weight of her body over to one side. Murky yelped as she tumbled through the air, and Laura screamed, but she managed not to drop directly into the fungus's throat. Instead she landed right on the lip, one half of her body dangling outside and the other inside, with her shirt catching and tearing on one of the tooth-like thorns.

"Murky, hang on!" Laura called up to her. "Whatever you do, don't fall in!"

"Um, it's not like that was on the top of my list of things to do," Murky muttered, but most of her concentration had to stay on her grip. This thing was incredibly slippery, and it was taking all of her effort not to tumble the rest of the way in. Although it was dark down in the gullet of the mushroom, she thought she could see some white spots that might have been the remains of bones.

"Look out!" Henderson called to her. She looked up just in time to see one of the vines whipping at her, obviously in an attempt to dislodge her and give the mushroom its meal. It barely missed her head, but a second one reared back, ready to hit her straight on. Murky closed her eyes, thinking this might very well be it, only to snap them back open again a second later as Chicago jumped at the tentacle and clawed the end of it right off, sending it flying into the mushroom's gullet. The fungus only barely reacted to this and certainly didn't seem to feel pain, but it did react when Chicago finished his absurdly high jump and landed right with his claws in the lip of the mouth. The entire mushroom swayed and shook violently in an effort to get the dinosaur off. Murky could feel her grip slipping, and she didn't think that she would be falling to the outside if she did.

"Chicago, help!" she called out to the velociraptor. In response, he opened his mouth and lunged his head at her, a movement that would have terrified her in any other circumstances. But instead of chomping down hard and killing her, he took her as gently as he could in his mouth and lifted her from the lip of the mushroom. The thorn that her shirt had been stuck on tore away with her and got caught between her and the dinosaur as they both tumbled away from the mushroom. Chicago let her go before they hit the spongey roots, keeping her from getting impaled by his teeth on impact.

Murky wanted to take a moment to hug and kiss the dinosaur in gratitude, but before she could, Laura was hauling her to her feet. "Come on! We've got to get out of here!"

They all ran past the mushroom as several more of the tentacles lashed at them, but now none of them came close to catching them. The element of surprise that it had had when it first attacked was gone, and the fungus couldn't do anything but reach out after them in vain as four kids and one dinosaur skipped out on their intended destiny as its dinner.

It was strange, but as they ran, Murky thought she could hear the mushroom make a weird creaking sound that was almost like a cry of rage.

CHAPTER NINE

They didn't stop running until they were far enough down their current tunnel to no longer see or hear any sign of the carnivorous mushroom. When they did stop, the four of them collapsed to the stone floor in exhaustion. Chicago, who had been limping along behind them, made a series of strange whining sounds as he too leaned his body against a wall for support.

"That was crazy," Jesse finally said when he got his breath back. "We seriously almost could have died."

"Murky," Laura said. When Murky looked over at her to see what she wanted, her big sister grabbed her in a tight hug and kissed the top of her head. "I thought I was about to lose you."

"Aw, don't be like that," Murky said, although she too had been terrified that she might not make it. "I'm perfectly okay."

"But are you?" Laura asked. She held Murky out at arm's length and looked her over as best she could in the dim green light. "What happened here?" she asked, indicating the huge gash in Murky's shirt. It wasn't positioned so the hole exposed anything embarrassing, but Murky felt self-conscious about it anyway.

"I got caught on one of those tooth things in that plant's mouth," Murky said.

"That *fungus's* mouth," Jesse corrected.

"Plant, fungus, whatever," Henderson said. "It was still something that shouldn't even *have* a mouth."

"Are you hurt?" Laura asked her. "There's... there's blood on you."

"What? Where?" Murky looked down at herself and saw that, yes, there was indeed a large smear of blood on her clothing, but when she checked herself, she couldn't find anywhere that the blood might be coming from. "I don't think this is mine."

"What, was it from the fungus?" Henderson asked. "Not only is this a place where mushrooms try to eat you, but you're telling me they actually bleed as well?"

"I don't think it's from the mushroom either," Jesse said. "Look." He pointed behind them. They'd been so caught up in their escape that none of them had noticed that Chicago, while still following them like a lost kitten, had fallen significantly behind. Once he limped closer, they could all see that he had to have been the source of the blood, as there was a fresh patch of it streaming down his leg.

"He must have gotten caught on the broken thorn while we were falling," Murky said.

"Do you think one of us should try to help him?" Jesse asked.

"Murky should," Laura responded. "She's the one with all the experience in taking care of animals."

"I take care of cats and hamsters," Murky said. "Those are really not even close to a dinosaur."

"Let me put it this way," Laura said. "Out of all of us, you're the one most likely to be gentle with him, and therefore the least likely to cause him pain."

Henderson snorted nervously. "And less likely to piss him off enough to want to eat us."

Jesse nodded. "You're also the smallest of us,

so you're the least likely to be appetizing."

"Okay, guys?" Laura said. "That's probably not helping her."

Murky cautiously approached Chicago, stopping once or twice when his whining became more of an angry growl. He didn't snap at her or otherwise try to keep her away, though.

"It's okay, Chicago. I just want to help you."

The dim glow of the wall fungus made it hard for her to see details until she got close, but the worst of his wounds seemed to be on his right leg. Everywhere else the damage looked like it was just small cuts, scrapes and scratches, but here the dinosaur's rough pebbled skin had been torn away in a deep gash. There was blood coming out of it, but not fast.

"Henderson, didn't you have your gym shirt in your backpack?" Murky asked.

"Why the hell would you want… oh, wait. I get it." He shrugged off his backpack and pulled out the gym shirt, causing all of them to wrinkle their noses in disgust at the smell as he handed it over. "Might not be the cleanest thing to put on an open wound, though."

"We are literally underneath the dirt," Jesse

said. "I don't think a little more grunginess is going to make the wound that much worse."

With Henderson's help, Murky tore the shirt into the longest strips she could manage and then set to wrapping them around Chicago's leg. The resulting bandage was pretty sad looking when it came to craftsmanship, but at least it covered up the entire wound and seemed to keep it from bleeding too much. All the while Chicago left Murky alone to do her work, although he did hiss at her several times when she was less than delicate with the wound. When she was finished, he shook his leg like he was trying to get the makeshift bandage off, then tried to nip at it with his teeth.

"Maybe we should put a cone around his neck to keep him from doing that," Murky said. "You know, like a dog."

"Murky, think for a second," Jesse said. "Where would we get one of those paper cone things down here in a cave?"

"Maybe we can find a way to make one out of your math book," Murky suggested.

"We don't have time to try being MacGyver just to give a dinosaur a cone around its neck," Laura said.

"Maybe we should make him stay behind," Henderson said. "If he's too badly hurt, he might slow us down."

"Uh-uh. No way," Jesse said. "He saved me. He could save us again if something else attacks us."

"Less than an hour ago none of us wanted him around, and now you're saying you have no problem with him?" Henderson asked.

"*I* wanted him around," Murky said quietly.

"Yeah, well, we were wrong," Jesse said. "He hasn't tried to attack us once, for some reason, and he was aware that something was wrong with the mushroom creature before any of us were. And we're still not even positive we're going the right way, but if he can sense danger then maybe he can help us figure out where the ant creatures went. And also? He saved us. We can't thank him by running off without him while he's hurt."

"I'm going to have to agree with them here," Laura said. "Chicago has proven pretty valuable, and if he hasn't killed and eaten us by now, then I kind of doubt he will."

They all looked at Henderson, who sighed. "Okay, fine. But I say it's Murky's responsibility to look after him and make sure he doesn't get us into trouble. That's fair, right?"

Murky enthusiastically shook her head. "Oh yeah. I can do that! I'll be good at it, too! I'll be the best dinosaur watcher ever!"

"You'll be the *only* dinosaur watcher ever," Jesse said. "At least the only human one."

"But Murky," Laura said, "you do realize that doesn't mean you get to keep him when we get back to the surface, right? Under no circumstances."

"Right. Of course. I understand," Murky said. But what she thought was *Oh my gosh, I'm going to keep him!*

"If he's up to walking again, we need to get going," Laura said.

"Any idea how much time we have left?" Jesse asked.

"Best guess? Somewhere between four and five hours, and even if we can find everyone, we still have to go all the way back the way we came."

"And we still don't even know if we're going on the right track," Henderson said morosely. "We could have been going down the wrong tunnels this whole time and we would have no way of knowing."

"Wait. What's that up ahead?" Murky asked.

She pointed at a spot some distance ahead where the tunnel flared out and appeared to go into another excessively large cavern like the one the dinosaurs had been in. The glow from there was far brighter than in the tunnel. Murky thought back to what Jesse had originally said about the glowing fungus being the source or large amounts of oxygen. If that was true, then it seemed possible that this might be a place that had something to do with the ant creatures that had taken the townsfolk. "That's got to be what we've been looking for, right?"

Before any of her companions could say otherwise, Murky ran for the mouth of the tunnel. Laura called out after her to stop, but Murky quickly heard the fast footsteps of three humans and one dinosaur running after her.

Murky skidded to a halt as soon as she was out of the tunnel, with Jesse so close behind her that he ran into her and almost knocked her over. They were on a ledge again like they had been in the dinosaur cave, and it gave them a perfect view of everything beyond.

"Okay, I'll admit I was wrong," Henderson said with hushed awe.

"About what?" Laura said with equal quiet.

"About what I just said," Henderson responded. "We were definitely headed the right way this entire time."

CHAPTER TEN

The only way to describe the structure they were seeing was as a city, but it was unlike any city that a human being had ever dreamed of living in. Hundreds of stalagmite-like spires reached up into the massive cavern, and while each one looked like it was made out of something like stone, the shapes were somehow organic. There were thousands of holes and balconies along the spires, none of them placed with any apparent rhyme or reason. From a number of them they could see some of the ant creatures scurrying out, easily gripping the sides as they went up and down the structures on tasks that the four of them couldn't even begin to imagine.

"That is so cool," Jesse said.

"And so big," Laura responded. "How are we going to find where they took the townsfolk?"

"If this even *is* where the ants took them,"

Henderson said.

"Make up your mind," Laura said. "First you say we went the wrong way, then you say we went the right way, and now you're back to where you started?"

"I don't know," Henderson said. "This is amazing, but for all we know there's hundreds of these city things down here."

"Um, I think this is the right place," Murky said. "Look down over there at that place that looks like it might be an entrance."

She pointed, and the rest looked in that direction. It appeared to be a weird color in the cavern's green glow, but there was a smear of something near the entrance that looked a lot like blood, and there were a few pieces that might have been torn-off human limbs, but thankfully they were too far into the shadows for them to see too many details.

Even in the cave's weird green glow, it was still easy to see Laura turn pale. "Is... is it anyone we know?"

"Looks like there might be some torn pieces of camo, so I'm thinking it's some of the soldiers that Agent Larson said they took before," Henderson said.

"So this is where the soldiers were taken," Jesse said. "But how do we know that the townsfolk were taken here as well?"

"And even if they were, where would we even begin to look?" Henderson asked. "This place is huge, and for all we know they stuffed everyone in a broom closet somewhere."

"I don't know," Laura said. "We're going to have to get in there and start searching for any clues."

"Okay, but how?" Henderson asked. "We would have to get past the guards."

"What guards?" Laura asked.

"Look right over there," Henderson said, pointing at a spot not too far from the tattered camo. It was in a corner with less of the glowing fungus, so it was hard to see at first, but there was indeed one of the ant creatures standing there. Murky had thought she'd be prepared to see one after the description they'd heard from Agent Larson, but it was completely a different thing when she finally saw one with her own eyes. In her mind she'd suspected something kind of cartoony, not the brown-carapace six-foot monster that was doing something like a patrol near the door. In almost all ways it looked like any other ant, or it would if real ants were the size of a motocross bike. Just as Agent Larson had said though, it had eight appendages instead of six, and its oversize mandibles included spikes that looked like it could impale someone if it ran headfirst into them. At the end of its top two pairs of legs it had small, thin claws like two thumbs right next to each other. In two of its hands it was carrying something long that looked like some kind of organically made spear, except with a large number of wicked-looking barbs and hooks at the end. It wasn't anything any one of them would want to face down, especially when they themselves didn't have anything at all that could be used as weapons. Well, not unless their dinosaur counted.

"I don't know if we would be able to get past that thing," Laura said. "There's also probably a lot more inside. This isn't looking very good for us."

Murky looked to Chicago. "What do you think? Do you have any ideas?"

Henderson gave an exaggerated sigh of exasperation. "Even if he was capable of having an idea, it's not like he could tell us."

Maybe not, but Murky couldn't help but notice

that something else farther away down the cavern had caught the velociraptor's interest. She followed his gaze down what almost looked like it could have been a road to see a number of large, strangely shaped green insects coming down it at a steady pace in single file.

"Hey look," Murky said, pointing at the line. "What's that?"

They all turned to look. The beginning of the line was some distance away, but it looked like it went on for quite a long way. The insects were nearly three times the size of the ants, but like the ants they had eight legs instead of six, more like a spider than an insect. Everything else about them though, made them look like nothing more than gigantic versions of bugs Murky had seen plenty of times out in the world.

"Those look like they could be this place's version of aphids," Jesse said.

"Isn't that what doctors call it when someone has a heart attack or something?" Henderson asked.

"That's *afib*, genius," Jesse said. "An aphid is an insect that has a symbiotic relationship with ants. Ants use them for nectar or something like that, and in turn the ants keep them safe from predators."

"So, uh, they're the ant version of dairy cows?" Murky asked.

"I, uh, I never thought of it that way," Jesse said. "But I guess that's kind of correct."

"So if those are supposed to be this dimension's version of aphids," Laura said, "then what are they doing right now?"

"They've got to eat if they're going to produce anything for the ants to feed on," Jesse said. "So I assume they're coming in from wherever the ants take them to graze. Like sheep or cows being let out into the pasture and then being taken back into the barn at night." He stared at the distant bugs intently, and Murky could tell that an idea was coming to him.

"If they're going to be heading into the city, maybe we can use them as cover to go inside as well," he said.

"How exactly would we do that?" Henderson asked.

"I'm not sure, but if we're going to try it, I think we have to get over by them now."

"He's right," Laura said. "If we're going to try to hide among them to get past that ant guard, we have to get among them before they're in easy sight of the entrance, and it looks like it will be pretty soon."

"There's a slope over there we can use," Henderson said. "Come on."

"Yeah, let's go," Murky said. She was about to gesture for Chicago to follow her when Laura stopped her with a hand on her shoulder.

"Murky, we can't bring Chicago with us this time. In fact, maybe it would be a good idea if you didn't come, either."

"What?" Murky asked. "Why?"

"We can't bring Chicago because he might scare the aphids," Laura said. "Not to mention that, however we're going to hide among them, Chicago's going to stick out and get us caught."

"That's not true," Murky said. "Chicago, you can pretend to be a bug, right?"

Chicago cocked his head at her. It didn't seem likely that he would agree in any case.

"And if he's going to stay behind, we probably need someone to keep an eye on him," Jesse said. "If the ants see him running around out here, it might tip them off that something is going on."

"You can do sentry duty," Laura said. "Keep an eye out for when we come out with the others."

"*If* we come out with the others," Henderson said. "Or at all."

Laura shook her head. "You're not helping, Henderson."

"Sentry duty," Murky said contemplatively. "That sounds pretty important. Is it?"

"Sure," Laura said. "Definitely."

"And you're not just trying to make me stay behind because of how dangerous it might be in there?"

"Of course not," Laura said. Something about the look on her face made Murky think she wasn't telling the truth, but she didn't mind. If it meant she got to stay here with Chicago, then she was fine with all of it.

"Okay. I'll do it."

"Good," Laura said. She hugged her little sister. "We'll be back as quick as we can, and hopefully with everyone from Kettle Hollow behind us."

The three of them snuck off down the nearest slope as quickly as they could. Murky turned to Chicago with a smile on her face.

"Sentry duty, Chicago!" she said. "This ought to be fun, right?"

Chicago's only response was to yawn.

CHAPTER ELEVEN

"Be honest," Henderson said to Laura as they quietly went down a path that they hoped would intercept the oncoming line of aphids while staying out of the view of the guards. "The reason you told Murky to stay behind is because you're not entirely sure we're going to make it in."

"No, that's not true," Laura said, then, softly added, "It's because I'm not sure we're going to make it *out*."

"At least I'm finally not the only pessimist here," Henderson said.

They met up with the line of aphids right around a corner from the colossal city, a perfect place to plan to set up their stealthy entrance without being seen. The only problem though, was they didn't have any idea what to do from here.

There were no ants or anything like that herding the aphids back to the city; they seemed to be doing that on their own purely out of instinct. But there was no doubt that any ants guarding the front gate would see them if they just walked with or crouched among the line of giant bugs. They didn't have a lot of time to come up with a plan, and Laura, who was tired and hungry and practically ready to collapse (and very much wishing she had grabbed a few of Murky's marshmallows before Chicago had consumed them all), found her thinking was getting muddy. Jesse, however, seemed to have a second wind.

"I wonder," he said aloud, then crouched down low to look at something underneath the bugs. "Yeah. Maybe that could work, if we can all hold on long enough."

"What do you mean?" Henderson asked.

Jesse gestured for the two others to stoop down along with him. "Take a look."

Laura got down on her hands and knees to look, but at first she wasn't sure what Jesse saw that had him so excited. "All I see are giant bug legs and giant bug bellies."

"Yeah, but look at their exoskeletons on the

underside."

Laura stared for a long time before she finally got it. "Those segments in the hard shell parts. We can use those as hand and footholds to hang from!"

"You want us to ride in underneath these things?" Henderson asked incredulously.

"One of these aphids by itself should be big enough to hold all three of us without us being easy to see from someone at normal eye height. Or abnormal ant height. Whatever."

"I think maybe we can do it," Laura said.

Henderson sighed and then shrugged. "What the hell. Why not. There could be worse ways to try to get in, right?"

He was singing a different tune, however, after the three of them had wriggled between one aphid's legs and positioned themselves to dangling from its underside. The line of aphids was getting very close to the gate now, but Henderson couldn't keep himself from getting his two cents in.

"These things totally smell like butt," he said. "Once we get back to Kettle Hollow, I'm going to have to burn these clothes. I'll never get the stink out."

"And yet it still smells better than your gym

shirt," Jesse whispered.

"Shh!" Laura said. "Not so loud. One of the guards might hear you."

As if on cue, one of the ant-men made a chittering noise and started moving towards their particular insect. Jesse started murmuring curse words quietly to himself.

"They're going to find us," he whispered. "This was a stupid idea!"

"It was *your* idea!" Henderson said.

"And it was a stupid one," Jesse said. "You two are the leaders. You're supposed to tell me when my ideas are stupid."

"Hey, I'm not the leader," Henderson said. "Blame that on Laura!"

"Who said I was the leader? Both of you just shut up or it will find us."

The guard came up around the outside of the giant bug, but Jesse noticed something about the way the ant creature was moving. "I don't think it can actually hear us," he said.

Laura looked for a moment like she was going to freak out at how loudly he said, but as the seconds passed, she and Henderson realized he was correct. From their current position they couldn't see much more than the ant creature's lower four legs, but it hadn't moved or reacted at all to Jesse's voice.

"Do ants even have ears?" Henderson asked.

"I don't think normal ants do, but these guys definitely don't," Jesse said.

"Then why is it investigating like it thinks something's wrong?" Laura asked.

They didn't dare move as the ant creature walked alongside the insect, moving back and forth as if it were agitated by something but not sure what. Finally, Jesse thought he had an answer. "It's the smell."

"Jesse, enough," Laura said. "Jokes about Henderson's gym shirt are just getting old now."

"No, I'm serious. I think that it can kind of detect we're here. But it can't be sure because these aphid things are that smelly."

The ant continued to pace back and forth in an agitated fashion. It never looked under the belly of the giant insect, but neither did it appear to be giving up on the idea that something was wrong. The aphid kept moving, but the attentions of the ant guard were slowing it down and causing the ones behind it to bump into it, jostling the three of them and threatening to make them lose their precarious grip on the creature's underbelly. If they didn't figure something out, they would be discovered long before the aphid got them through the entrance to the city.

"You said they can't hear," Laura said. "Are you sure that's true?"

"I mean, kind of," Jesse said. "I don't think they really hear. It's more like they can sense vibrations. He's probably not sensing the vibrations of us talking because it's being hidden by the vibrations of the bug's legs on the stone."

"Then I think I've got an idea," Laura said. Being careful to keep her feet and one hand braced against the bug's scaly underside, she reached over to Jesse and started to unzip his backpack. He started to protest but stopped when she carefully, without letting anything else fall out, pulled out his math textbook.

"What are you doing?" Henderson said to her. He didn't seem to realize he was still whispering, regardless of whether or not the ant guard could hear him.

"Creating vibrations, and doing it away from us," Laura said. She hefted the textbook a couple of times in her hand, testing to see its weight, and then flung it like a really heavy frisbee out in a direction behind them, away from the current position of the guard. The throw was awkward from her upside-down angle, but the book flew far enough to hit one of the walls with a hefty thumping noise.

It worked far better than any of them could have imagined. At the sound, the ant ran off after it, leaving their aphid to go back on its path with no more interruptions. The ant that had been investigating them wasn't the only one who went after the sound, either. Several other guards that they hadn't seen came scurrying from various shadowed places and jumped on the math book with savage ferocity. It seemed that none of them were now paying any attention to the aphids as the bugs marched through the gate, including the one with its three intruders hanging from its underside.

Jesse stared back at the guards ripping his math book to shreds, then looked at Laura. "Do you think she'll believe me?"

"Do I think who will believe what?" Laura asked.

"My math teacher. Do you think she'll believe me when I tell her that ants ate my homework?"

Henderson snickered and Laura had to hold

back a laugh of her own. It might have been easier to appreciate the humor if they weren't riding on the underside of a giant insect on their way into a hostile nest of human-sized killer ants.

The inside of the structure had the kind of waxy, papery texture to the walls that Laura associated with a wasp's nest, although the material looked like it might be more durable. At regular intervals along the walls there were concentrated patches of the glowing fungus, obviously grown there on purpose to provide light like torches in sconces in a medieval castle.

"Okay, so now we're in," Henderson said. "What are we supposed to do from here?"

"Well, first we're probably going to have to ditch our ride," Laura said. "I don't know where exactly these things are going in here, but it's probably not going to be the same place we want to go."

Henderson let go of the aphid's underside first and rolled out from between the legs before they could trample all over him. Laura and Jesse went at the same time but weren't as graceful. While they didn't end up getting trod on by the bug, they did trip it a little and cause it to walk slightly off the path that the others were following. As if suddenly confused, it stepped aside to let the other aphids pass and began to turn in a circle like it wasn't sure where to go next.

"I think you guys broke it," Henderson said.

"It doesn't matter," Laura said. "We need to get moving."

They started to make their way down the various halls and found that the bug, very much like Chicago had done, was now following them. However, whereas Chicago had almost seemed to be doing it with a true sense of purpose, the aphid appeared to be doing because it had no idea what else it was supposed to do.

"Okay, so now where are we supposed to go?" Henderson asked. "The whole 'follow the glowing fungus' thing worked to get us here, but I don't think that would be the best way to find our way around inside this place."

"Well, I'm going to start by heading toward the noise," Laura said. "Don't you hear that? It sounds like there's a bunch of those ant things in one place."

"Somehow that does not reassure me," Jesse said. "Under normal circumstances, I would say that wherever there are a large number of giant mutant ants from another dimension, that would be some place that I don't want to be."

"Yeah, but these aren't normal circumstances," Henderson said. "Come on."

There were a number of winding halls going every which way as well as rooms that held nothing and had no apparent reason for existing, but it was easy to follow the sounds of chittering and the clacking of ant legs on the hard surface. On occasion they had to stop and hide in some alcove when they thought one of the ant people were coming, but at no point were they discovered. Here, the aphid following them and bumping around into things seemed to be a sort of advantage, as its smell must have continued to mask them. Any of the ants that saw the aphid alone looked at it strangely, but apparently that wasn't enough of an unusual sight to make them suspicious. Jesse lingered every so often behind them, obviously fascinated by the structure around them.

"It's a shame we don't have time to explore more," Jesse said. "Imagine all the things we could learn from this place."

"It's a gigantic pile of hardened mud,"

Henderson said. "What's there to learn?"

"You just don't have any sense of the academic," Jesse said.

"What is that even supposed to mean?" Henderson asked.

"Would you two just hush?" Laura said. "I think we're getting closer. There's something brighter up ahead."

They ascended a set of stairs with the same peculiar proportions as the ones they had gone down after going through the portal and found themselves on some kind of balcony overlooking a great hall. There were another set of stairs that led down from it into the main portion of the room, but none of them dared go down them yet. The source of the noise was obviously coming from down there, and none of them wanted to head right in without getting a better idea of what was going on. With the aphid still sitting behind them, the three of them got low and peered over the edge.

There was immediately no doubt that they were in the right place. The room contained every person from Kettle Hollow, although it took them a few seconds to really understand what was happening to them. Everyone was in some state of being covered by a resin-like cocoon. Some were almost completely covered except for their mouths and noses, while others only had the bare minimum needed to keep them from moving. They were lined up in long lines atop raised sections of the floor, and the ants were swarming around them, some poking the townspeople like they were checking if they could move and some continuing to add the resin substance on top of anyone still struggling. Many of the humans, especially most of the children, were crying and sobbing or begging to be let free.

"What are those things doing to them?" Henderson asked in horror.

"Um, guys? Take a look over there," Laura said. She pointed at a farther point in the room where something similar was set up, but it was obvious that none of the humans that had been in that part of the room were alive. Instead most of the resin cocoons were broken and filled with bones and blood and gore. Multiple scraps of camo told them that this was where the rest of the soldiers that had been taken from Project Subterranea had met their fate. In a couple of spots some of the ants were still swarming over the cocoons and chewing on the remains inside, even though there wasn't much left.

Jesse gasped and Henderson looked like he would be sick as they all realized what this place was. The upraised portions of the floor were the ant versions of dining tables. This was a banquet hall, and the townsfolk of Kettle Hollow were being prepared as tonight's main course.

CHAPTER TWELVE

Jesse started to stand up and head toward the stairs, but Henderson grabbed him by the back of his shirt. "Where the hell do you think you're going?"

"Are you blind?" Jesse asked. "Don't you see what's going to happen? They're going to eat them!"

"So? Most of the people down there hate me." There was a quaver in Henderson's voice, however, that told Jesse and Laura that he was very much disturbed by the possibility.

"If we just go running down there with so many ant-men around, all they're going to do is capture us," Laura said. "And then we'll be pizza for the ants as well."

"Do ants even eat pizza?" Henderson asked.

"Ants eat everything," Jesse said.

"None of this is helping," Laura said. She looked back over her shoulder at the giant green insect, which was still just standing around like it had no idea what to do with itself. "I've got an idea. We can cause a distraction and get most of the guards away from the eating area."

"So what, we just send that thing running down there?" Henderson asked. "How are we supposed to do that? We don't know that it'll lead them away or not."

"That's why we don't send it by itself. We send it down with someone riding it."

"And who the hell would be dumb enough to do that?" Henderson asked.

Both Jesse and Laura turned to look right at him. It took him a moment to understand.

"Wait, what?" Henderson asked.

"Out of all of us, you're the best BMX rider," Laura said. "You would be the best one to ride it down, confuse the hell out of all the ant people, and then run on out with all of them chasing after you."

"Excuse me, but how the hell are you thinking *that's* similar to a BMX?" Henderson asked, pointing at the giant green bug.

Laura pointed at its antennae. "Those are *sort of* like handlebars."

Henderson shook his head. "No. They're really not."

"Just imagine it's a Murray or a Mongoose," Laura said. "I've seen the way you can handle a bike. Handling a giant bug can't be that much different."

"You guys are crazy," Henderson said. But both Laura and Jesse could see the look in his eye as he started to imagine himself on top of the creature. He was probably thinking of how to do jumps and wheelies with it, if such a thing could even be done with a giant bug. "Okay, so if I did try this, and that's a really big if, what would the plan be?"

"It looks like there's stairs that lead down there over to the right," Laura said. "You get on the aphid, steer it down those stairs, cause a ruckus among the ants, and then use the bug to run out of the room and draw the ants with you. Once all or most of them are away, Jesse and I can run down there and free everybody."

"And what happens after that?" Henderson asked. "What happens when you have several hundred people trying to run out of the dining room and the city of a race of giant ant people?"

"How the hell should I know?" Laura said. "I've been playing this whole thing by ear since we came down here. If you've got a problem with my planning skills, then maybe you can come up with something better?"

"Hey, calm down, okay?" Henderson said. "I was just wondering. And no, I don't have anything better." He looked again at the giant aphid standing behind them like it was waiting for someone or something to give it orders. "Okay. Let's go for it." He went over to the bug and felt along the sides of it for handholds he could use to climb onto its back. "It's a shame none of us have a camcorder, because I'm totally betting I'd be able to send a VHS of this to get on a pro BMX team."

With some effort, Henderson was able to climb up on top of the insect's back. It didn't start to get skittish until he came close to its head. "All right," Henderson said. "Give me a minute or two to get used to this before we do it. Let's see. No pedals to control the speed but if I do this…"

He grabbed the antennae, and instantly the aphid went berserk. Before he could do anything resembling gaining control of the creature, it ran right for the edge of the ledge and leaped off into the large dining chamber below. Henderson's scream started out as one of terror, but even as the bug landed in the room below and startled all the ants swarming around getting ready for dinner, the sound evolved into a sound of joy and taunting.

"Hey, numbnuts!" he yelled at the ants. "If you think those people look tasty, you should get a load of me! Come on, you know you want some of this!" Laura couldn't tell if he managed to steer the bug around or if was just spinning in confusion and fear, but the aphid bolted for a large gateway. After a moment of shock and confusion, all of the ants in the room ran after it.

"It worked," Jesse said. "How in the hell did that actually work?"

"Let's not question it," Laura said. "Come on. We probably don't have a lot of time before some of them decide chasing Henderson down isn't the best way to be spending their time."

They ran down the slope into the dining hall and took a quick look around at the many captives. A few of them might have been asleep or unconscious, but it didn't look like any of them were dead. If the ants really were planning on eating them, they looked like they had intended on doing it with their prey still alive and wriggling. Many of them had the weird resin-like substance over their mouths to keep them from talking, but a few that didn't saw them and started shouting for help.

"Shh!" Laura said. "The ants will hear you."

Most of them quieted down at that, but one particular voice kept talking. "Laura? Laura, honey, is that you?"

Laura turned to the sound of the voice and gasped. "Mom? Dad?"

Her parents were cocooned to the "dining table" a couple spaces over from each other. Her mom was too covered up to move or speak, but her father's head was completely uncovered, and he became noticeably emotional at seeing her. "Laura! You need to get out of here, or they'll get you too."

"I'm not going anywhere. We came all the way down here to rescue all of you." Laura ran up to her father and began working at the cocoon. The hardened substance was enough to keep the people immobile, but she found that with a lot of work she could chip away at it. Looking around for some kind of tool she could use to help her, all she found was a few chunks of grisly human bones. She shuddered quietly to herself but otherwise didn't hesitate to grab one and use it to hammer the resin until her father was able to break the rest of the way free by himself. He immediately found something else hard, and the two of them worked to free Laura's mom as well while Jesse made a beeline for his own mother.

"Where's Murky?" Laura's mother asked once her mouth was free.

"She's outside this city," Laura said. "She's waiting with our, um, dinosaur."

Her father looked at her with bewilderment, but he didn't seem to disbelieve her. "There's dinosaurs down here as well as monster insects?"

"Yeah, and a lot of other things," Laura said. "Why? Didn't any of you see them as the ants were taking you down here?"

"There wasn't a lot that we could see, with how fast they moved us," Laura's mom said. "I think they took us on a different path than you went. What is even going on? What is this place?"

"It's a long story that we'll have to tell later, after we get back to the surface," Laura said. "The ants haven't killed anyone yet, have they?"

"Not anyone from Kettle Hollow that I've seen so far," her father said. "Those soldiers that were here before us, though…"

"There's nothing we can do for them now," Laura said. "But we have to free the rest of the townsfolk before the ants realize that Henderson and his BMX bug are just a distraction."

The work of freeing them was frustratingly slow at first, and Laura was worried for several minutes. But each new person they freed helped free the others, and soon everyone from Kettle Hollow was out of their resin cocoons and ready for someone to tell them what to do next. Laura realized with a start that most of them were waiting on her. She had expected that once she got them free she would no longer have to be the one taking on the leadership. Except none of them knew how to get out of here, and Laura and Jesse did.

"Um, let's go," she said to hundreds of people milling around looking for someone to guide them. "We should be able to get out the way we came."

"Wait," someone said. He had to push his way through the crowd before Laura realized it was Henderson's father. "What about my son? Where did he go?"

That was a really good question, and one Laura wasn't entirely prepared to answer. But while she hadn't been too self-conscious about leading her three friends, she was suddenly very much aware that she could look unworthy to all these people if she didn't think her response through carefully.

So she lied. "We have a plan." She immediately felt bad about it, and her parents, both of whom knew her well enough, exchanged glances that told her she wasn't fooling them. "Henderson is going to meet us out in front of the main gate."

Before anyone could call her on her fib, she pointed them all in the direction of the stairs and had them go up, staying as close together as possible in the hopes that a tighter group would be less likely to be discovered.

They didn't get very far. Only two turns back down the direction they had come, they found Henderson, but Henderson wasn't alone. The aphid he'd been riding had been impaled with one of the ants' spears, and a large group of the ants surrounded him and were moving in to attack. They turned at the approach of the townsfolk, and she could see that, even though they outnumbered the ants by quite a bit, there wasn't a lot of chance that they were going to escape this.

At least Murky's not here for this, Laura thought. *I hope she and that silly dinosaur realize what's going on and run as far away from here as possible.*

The ants chittered a battle cry, then ran at the petrified people of Kettle Hollow.

CHAPTER THIRTEEN

"So, uh, how do you like being a dinosaur?"

It was impossible for Murky to be sure, but the way the velociraptor tilted its head made her think that it might also really understand her question. Chicago didn't do anything in the way of a response, however. Murky decided to take that as a sign that it was okay to continue.

"I've met all kinds of animals, but you're the first dinosaur I ever met," Murky said. "Uh, obviously. It's not like there's a lot of you running around in my world."

The dinosaur huffed, then turned its head around to scratch its back with its teeth. It was a very bird-like gesture that Murky never would have thought a dinosaur would do.

"Do you think you would like it up top with us?

You could come live at my house."

She didn't actually think that would be a plausible situation. It was nice to think about though, although it wouldn't do her much good if she didn't have a house or family to go back to.

Murky leaned back against the cave wall and stared at the ceiling. Sure, she was supposed to be watching the entrance to the strange ant city, but nothing of interest had happened since the giant aphids had gone in. "Wow. Sentry duty is really boring."

Chicago suddenly tensed and sniffed the air. Murky snapped her head back to look at the entrance, but she didn't immediately see anything that might have alarmed the dinosaur. "Did you hear something?" Murky asked him. "Or smell something?"

The dinosaur growled in a way that was very familiar. It took Murky a moment to realize this was the same kind of noise he had made right before they'd been attacked by the carnivorous mushroom.

"Is there something dangerous down there?" Murky asked. "Are the others in trouble? Maybe we should go help." The more she thought about it, the more it seemed like a good idea to go down there even if the others weren't in trouble yet. Surely they would be soon, and once they were, she would need to be ready.

"You're right. We should *definitely* go help. How's your leg doing? Do you feel well enough for me to try something?" Again, Chicago made no coherent response, but neither did he try to pull away as Murky went right up next to him and began rubbing a hand on his back. "Your back seems pretty strong, and I'm pretty light. Do you think I would be able to ride you?"

Chicago made no movements or sounds that she could interpret as either positive or negative, so she decided to just assume that meant yes. It took her several awkward seconds to try swinging her leg over Chicago's back, but he did seem to lower his body a little as though he were trying to help her get on easier. She'd never ridden on any kind of animal before, so she wasn't sure if she was even astride it right, but she did know she was supposed to have some kind of reins, and there just wasn't anything that would work.

"If I hold on really tight to your neck to keep from falling off, is that going to make you angry?"

Chicago's only response was to sneeze.

"Okay, so how do we do this? Am I supposed to say 'giddy-up?' Do you even know what that means?" He didn't seem to, so instead Murky tried to think back to all the times she had seen people ride horses in movies. She thought they did something with their ankles or heels to get their rides moving. Gently, she dug her heals into Chicago's sides.

She had expected him to start along at a slow walk or trot, if he moved at all. Instead he took off immediately down the rough, rocky slope that the others had gone down, and Murky had to clutch his neck hard to stay balanced. It seemed like he was helping her though, shifting his body beneath her to keep her at the center of his back and preventing her from falling off. Murky would have tried to steer him, but honestly she had no idea how to do that or even where exactly they wanted to go. Chicago seemed to have an idea of his own about what they needed to do, and Murky was just along for the ride.

Chicago sprinted along the path to the same gate that the aphids had gone through and reached it just as one of the guards was coming out. It looked confused, like it wasn't sure if it should be running from the dinosaur or attacking, but Chicago never gave it the chance to do either. Instead he snapped his jaws at the ant's abdomen, and to Murky's surprise and awe, the bite was strong enough to rip the ant guard in half at the waist (if ants could even be said to have a waist). The two halves hit the ground and twitched independently of each other for several seconds before finally going still. For someone like Murky, who genuinely found any life at all to be fascinating, it was a disturbing thing to watch, even if it was just an insect.

It also made her glad Chicago was on her side rather than theirs.

From inside the gate, Murky could now hear what might have been shouts or screams. A lot of them definitely sounded human, but many others were chittering and screeching that Murky could only assume were the ants. She would have urged Chicago inside to investigate, but she didn't need to. He dashed through the gate all by himself, snarling at any of the ants that got too close and ripping holes in their shells with his powerful claws if they got too close.

They didn't get far down the initial hall of the city before they ran into the scuffle that had been causing all the racket and alerted Chicago. There was a fight going on between the ants and the people of Kettle Hollow, and while the townsfolk didn't seem to be armed with anything but a couple of jagged bones, they weren't putting up too bad of a fight. Lots of children, and even a few adults, were screaming and cowering in fear, but most of them were going bare-knuckled into battle, knowing that their lives literally depended on it. But even though the people looked like they were making the ants work for every ounce of spilled blood, it was obvious that they wouldn't be able to continue on like this for long.

"Good thing I've got a velociraptor, then," Murky said aloud to no one in particular. "Chicago, charge!"

She dug her heels into the dinosaur's sides and spurred him forward, but he did all of the rest of the work. Murky wouldn't have known where to even begin when attacking astride a velociraptor, but Chicago's instincts took over and he ripped through a large number of the ants before they even realized that they were now fighting a battle on two sides. Some of the ants shrieked and made smells that Murky assumed were their version of orders to retreat, but there weren't many places for them to go. They were caught in a pincer between the dinosaur and the townsfolk, and they were getting crushed in between.

"Murky!" she heard Laura call out from on the other side of the ants. "I told you to stay put!"

"I got bored!" she said honestly, then, less honestly, "and also, Chicago got worried and wouldn't let me stay behind."

"Murky!" Henderson called. "Get Chicago to back up!"

"But if I do that, the ants will be able to move this way!"

"Duh! And so will we!"

"Oh. Right. Got it," Murky said. The problem was, she wasn't sure *how* to make a dinosaur she was riding back up. Was there something she was supposed to say? Was she supposed to try to lead him around? She touched him on the top of the head and tried to turn it back the direction they had come, which thankfully he seemed to understand. He whipped his tail around to take out a few more ants, then started running down the hall back to the gate. Most of the townsfolk followed immediately, although some were obviously hesitant about following something that looked like a giant wingless bird of prey. There were ants starting to come from back in the direction where they had just been though, and that convinced the stragglers to fight their way past the remaining ants in their path.

Chicago and Murky burst out of the gate with the people close behind them, and Chicago immediately went for the path he had originally come down. At the top, Murky managed to get him to stop moving long enough to let her off and find Laura, who gave her the warmest, tightest hug the two sisters had ever shared. The townspeople came to a stop, milling around on the ledge and the slope, most of them anxiously looking back at the gate of the giant ant city as though expecting an army to come pouring out after them.

After waiting a number of moments and the ants still hadn't done so, even Murky began to feel uneasy. A couple of ants came out to look at them, but as soon as they saw the direction the townspeople were heading, they ran back inside as though they were the ones that were scared.

"Laura, why does something about this give me a bad feeling?" Murky asked.

"I don't know," Laura said. "But that feeling? I've got it, too."

CHAPTER FOURTEEN

The townspeople all went at least far enough down the tunnels to be out of eyesight of the ant city, and it was there that they finally took a moment to express their relief, as well as where Murky got to have her reunion with her parents. After a few minutes, Mr. Turnbull, the grouchy pharmacist, came up to the head of the group and started speaking. "Now that we're out of there, let's go." He started walking and most of the people followed, although Laura, Murky, Jesse, and Henderson all took umbrage at his attitude.

"You don't need to be a jerk about it, Turnbull," Henderson said.

"The hell I don't," Mr. Turnbull said. "I'll be damned if I have to follow a little punk like you any more than I have to."

"Hey, we're the ones that came all the way down here by ourselves and then kept every one of you from being ant food, didn't we?"

Mr. Turnbull shook his head. "Probably despite your own best efforts at failing, I'm sure."

"Hey!" Henderson's father grabbed Mr. Turnbull by the shoulder and gripped the older man tightly. "That's my son you're speaking to, and he just saved us. If you keep speaking to him like that, I can make sure you get un-saved really quick."

Henderson's jaw dropped as he stared at his father in amazement. "Dad?"

Henderson's dad looked at him with a combination of sadness and joy. "I'm proud of what you did today, George. If we don't get out of this, I just want you to know that."

Murky didn't think she had ever seen Henderson look that close to crying, but he quickly hid it before anyone else could see.

Several young men had been carrying old Mrs. Harmsen, who normally needed a wheelchair, but they called out for the others to stop. "We have to take a break," one of them said. "I'm not used to carrying an entire person this far."

"I need a break from him as well," Mrs. Harmsen said. "This young man smells funny. He smells like, before we were taken, he might have been…"

"We can't stop," Laura said to them. "I don't know exactly how long we've been down here, but we have a time limit." She gave everyone listening a brief version of everything Agent Larson had told them about what was going on, ending with the imminent threat of the military forcing the portal closed with them all on the wrong side.

"I highly doubt that's true," Mr. Turnbull said.

"If my kids say it's true, then I believe them," Murky and Laura's mom said.

A younger kid came up to Murky and tugged on her shirt. "How do we get out?" he asked.

"Just follow us," Murky said. "We'll lead the way. We know which direction we came from. We just need to take a left at the giant carnivorous mushroom, then go up and to the right after the dinosaur cavern."

"It was up and to the left at the dinosaurs."

"It was definitely to the right."

Harry Lupin, who managed the local Piggly Wiggly, gaped at them and scoffed. "Dinosaurs? Killer mushrooms? You have to be making that up."

Henderson gave him an exasperated look. "Seriously, did you or did you not see that we're travelling with our own velocity ratter?"

"That's velociraptor," Jesse corrected.

"Whatever. It's obviously a dinosaur and it's walking right next to us. Please tell me that not everyone becomes stupid like that when they become an adult."

There was a lot of petty bickering after that, but none of the adults tried to act like they were in charge anymore. They could be in charge again once they all made it back to the surface. For the moment it was the four kids that had found their way down here, and they were the only four who knew exactly how to get back.

Murky thought they probably made quite the sight, an entire small town's worth of people walking through the glowing green caves. A lot of them had been injured when the ants took them, but no one dared slow down after what Laura had said.

Henderson gestured for them all to slow down a little as they got closer to the place where they'd encountered the killer mushroom. "I don't think we've thought enough about this," he said to Laura. "How are we going to get past that thing again with so many people this time? The first time we barely made it through with our lives."

"I'm still just making up all of this as we go," Laura said to him in a conspiratorial whisper. "Maybe Chicago will be able to help us again."

Except, once they got back to the place where they clearly remembered fighting the killer mushroom, they found it gone. Except it wasn't *completely* gone. There were still pieces of it, especially chunks of the rubbery tentacles and root-like structure. But most of the giant fungus was gone, and it didn't look like it had somehow got up and walked by itself. There were clear signs of violence. Various tendrils looked like they had been ripped apart by something large and strong, and there was a disgusting goo on the ground in places that Murky thought might have been the liquid she'd seen in the mushroom's stem.

"Something bad happened here," Murky muttered. Chicago made a soft noise in response that almost could have been agreement.

"Doesn't seem so bad to me," Henderson said. "Anything that gets rid of that monster plant has to be good for us."

"Monster *fungus*," Jesse corrected. "And I don't know. Whatever did this, it could still be around. And do you really want to meet something that could completely destroy a creature that almost killed us so easily?"

The four of them agreed that they didn't, but none of them told any of the others that something capable of ripping up giant monster mushrooms might be lurking around. Instead they continued on, again expecting some rather interesting reactions from the townsfolk when they came to the cavern of the dinosaurs. But that was empty too, even if it didn't seem to be the sight of some kind of fight like the space where the mushroom had been.

"Where did they all go?" Murky asked, half to her friends and half to Chicago.

"There's a few of these tunnels that look like they might be big enough for the dinosaurs to hide in," Jesse said. "But I'm betting it wouldn't be a comfortable fit."

"So they all ran away," Henderson said. "What exactly could be so scary that it could make a tyrannosaurus run away screaming in fear?"

"I don't know, but it's not something I want to meet," Laura said.

"Hey," one of the townsfolk said. "You kids mind telling the rest of us what you're whispering to each other that is making you turn so pale?"

"Oh, nothing," Laura said. Unfortunately, Murky was pretty sure everyone could tell she was lying. Being the typical good girl that she was, Laura didn't have a lot of practice at being convincing when she lied.

"We just need to get moving, is all," Henderson said. From him, a lie sounded much more convincing. "We don't have much further to go, but we're probably really short on time."

Even though every single person in their very long train was tired, exhausted and traumatized, they all picked up their pace. It wasn't until they passed the shattered remains of Agent Larson's communicator device that Murky began to have a suspicion, and it was one that her three main companions obviously shared with her.

"The thing we saw in this tunnel," Murky whispered to them, "I think maybe that's what ripped apart the mushroom."

"And scared away the dinosaurs," Jesse said.

"And also probably why the ants aren't trying to chase after their dinner," Henderson added. "Whatever it is, it's something they didn't want to mess with."

"Do we still not have any idea what it even

was?" Murky asked.

"I don't know," Jesse said. "Maybe. We've got giant ants and giant aphids. Based on that and what we were able to see of the creature when it passed, I have an idea, but I'd rather not say it. I kind of hope I'm wrong."

"Oh come on," Henderson said to him. "You can't just leave us hanging like that. Tell us what you're thinking."

"Have you ever heard of an ant-lion?" Jesse asked.

"No," Henderson responded.

Somewhere behind them, deep within the caverns, they heard an ungodly screech much like the one they had heard when they'd first come down. Everyone from town turned to look in the direction of the sound with terror on their faces.

"You may not have heard *of* one," Jesse said, "but I think you just *heard* one. Everyone, I think maybe it's time to run!"

Even though an entire town's worth of people started running down the tunnel, it wasn't the sort of panicked free-for-all that one might have expected. No one trampled anyone else, and no one was left behind. Children too small to run effectively were picked up, multiple people assisted with Mrs. Harmsen, and anyone who fell was given a hand up and a push to keep them going. Even with each of them helping each other though, some just couldn't move as fast as others. A few near the end were struggling. Murky, with Chicago by her side, went to the back to help. Jesse and Henderson went with her, and Laura came back just as the front portion of the group reached the bottom of the deep pit that would lead them back to their own dimension.

"The portal's still open!" Laura said. "We may still have a chance to do this."

"Um, I don't think we're going to have that chance for much longer," Henderson said. "Look!"

He pointed back down the tunnel. Something was coming, something huge. Something that blocked the light behind it. Something with giant, over-sized mandibles at the front of its head.

Something that was going to be here any second.

CHAPTER FIFTEEN

Laura got separated from the others on the desperate run up the stairs, so she somehow ended up near the front of the line of townspeople as they spilled out over the glowing blue edge of the portal. It was tough to tell who was more surprised: the townspeople who suddenly had guns stuck in their faces, or the soldiers, who had given the town up for dead and were now surrounding the portal, doing whatever preparations they needed to blow it closed. There was some frantic shouting from the soldiers, but it stayed fairly organized until the unholy scream of a monster echoed up from the bottom of the hole and caused both military and civilian alike to start running away from the edge in chaos.

The vast majority of the townspeople got out of

the hole and over the edge of the portal before the creature came up. Murky wasn't sure which direction to run, so instead she just stayed near Chicago and let his fearsome snarl scare away anyone that came close to trampling her. Mr. Turnbull ended up being the last one on the stairs, but he never got a chance to step over the blue line that separated the dimensions. The monster came up behind him and snatched him up in its jaws before rearing up and giving everyone in town a clear view of the thing that had been pursuing them.

Murky had never seen an ant-lion before, so she could only assume that Jesse was right in his assumption that this was some kind of cosmic mutant version of one. It towered almost two stories over everyone, and that was with a significant portion of it still down in the hole. It was mostly insectoid, but just like the ants and aphids, it had more legs than it was supposed to. Unlike the other extra-dimensional bugs though, it had at least ten legs that Murky could see. But the truly terrifying aspect of the creature, the part they had only gotten the barest hint of earlier, were its massive, out-of-proportion mandibles clicking at the air. The mandibles crushed Mr. Turnbull into paste, allowing the creature to more easily consume its prey.

Chicago growled next to her. He almost looked like he was aware that Murky was in danger and didn't want to let anything happen to her. He took several steps forward, putting himself between her and the beast.

"Chicago, no! Please don't do it!"

There was no doubt about it this time. As the velociraptor turned its head to look at her, Murky was positive that it completely understood what she was saying, or at least the sentiment behind her words. It even did something that might have been a response this time, a guttural and sad sound from deep in its throat. Then it turned back to the massive ant-lion and hissed a clear challenge.

The creature finished gulping down Mr. Turnbull, then started scanning the running townsfolk for its next victim. Multiple soldiers were running toward the portal, their guns firing, but none of the bullets seemed to phase the enormous ant-lion. Chicago rushed up to the swirling glow at the edge of the portal and jumped, his mouth wide and ready to snap. His jaw latched tight and hard on one of the ant-lion's legs, causing an audible crack of chitin to be heard. The ant-lion screeched and shook its leg, but Chicago held tight.

"It's distracted!" one of the soldiers yelled. "Everyone, aim for the head and eyes!"

The air erupted with gunfire, and Murky screamed as she saw one or two errant shots hit Chicago. Even though the dinosaur winced and flailed in pain, he still held on, and the ant-lion was so preoccupied with him that it seemed to barely notice the bullets hitting it.

While the townsfolk ran screaming in terror and the soldiers confusedly shot at anything that didn't seem human, Laura saw Agent Larson trying to command several troops off to one side and ran toward her. Larson saw her coming and tried to wave her away.

"Kid, this is seriously not the best time."

"You said something earlier about ordinance to close the portal," Laura said. "You have to use it now!"

"Are you crazy? The plan was to destroy the entire town, and to do it from a distance. We can't do it while everyone is still right here!"

"If you don't do it or something like it, then that ant-lion thing is going to escape and get out into the world," Laura said. "If you've got the means to blow it up, it might be better to try doing it now than if it makes a beeline for Milwaukee or Green Bay!"

As if in response, the ant-lion pulled its enormous body up further out of the hole and used one of its legs to swipe at a group of more official looking soldiers. One of them tried to call out an order, but before he could complete it, they were all swept aside and flung through the air, some of them right into the ant-lion's snapping mandibles.

Agent Larson turned to one of the nearest soldiers. "Get some grenades, or anything else explosive that we can set around the portal. We still might be able to interrupt the portal's frequency with something smaller than we originally planned."

Murky continued to scream at Chicago as he refused to let go of the creature, which was finally forced to turn all of its attention to the dinosaur. It raked its huge mandibles against the leg Chicago was chomping, an act that succeeded in dislodging the dinosaur but also tore off a large portion of its own leg. The cry the ant-lion gave was unearthly, unlike anything they had ever heard before, but Laura took it as a good sign that maybe they might be able to win this. A couple of soldiers ran forward with open crates of what Laura assumed had to be the explosives, although to her they looked more like ropes made out of some kind of long, thin, clay-like material. "Um, is this stuff really explosive?" Laura asked as she gingerly pulled one out and held it up where she could see it.

"It's something experimental," one of the soldiers said. To Laura's surprise, he didn't make a fuss about the fact that a teenager with no military experience was handling a volatile substance. Instead he showed her how to stick the detonators into each of the ropes. "You don't need to worry about setting it off. That can only be done by remote."

While Laura was preoccupied with that, Henderson found himself next to a similar crate as it was opened. But instead of the strange explosives, this one had a large number of grenades. "Oh hell yeah!" Henderson said and reached in to grab a handful, startling the soldier that had opened the crate.

"Wait, kid, what are you doing?" he asked. "You can't just…"

"Watch me!" Henderson said, then ran in the

direction of the portal and the giant ant-lion. The soldier didn't seem to know whether he should be trying to stop him or direct him about the best place to throw the weapons. Henderson, however, was smart enough to not just go tossing the hand grenades willy-nilly at the ant-lion. With his luck it would probably hit the creature's chitin and then bounce back to explode in his face. Instead he looked for a large spot between the edge of the portal and the ant-lion's body where he would be able to chuck the grenades, some place where their explosions wouldn't shower the townsfolk and soldiers in shrapnel.

While Henderson, with assistance from Jesse, started lobbing the grenades down the portal like they were basketballs, Murky ran over to the spot where Chicago had been thrown to the ground some distance from the raging battle. "Chicago! Please, please be okay!"

But she could tell just from a quick look at him that he was not going to be okay at all. The leg that she had previously wrapped up with Henderson's gym shirt was twisted at a sickening angle, and there were gashes and cuts all over him that bled profusely. This wasn't something she would be able to patch up with torn pieces of clothing this time, and she doubted there was a veterinarian in the area who was practiced with healing damaged velociraptor anatomy.

Still, she didn't want to give up on him just yet. "Come on, Chicago. Get up. We can still get you somewhere safe. Just get up and I promise I'll take care of you for as long as I live."

Chicago looked at her, and there was absolutely no doubt in her mind that he knew what she was trying to say, whether he understood her language or not. If there was something he wanted to say back to her though, it was beyond his abilities. He was at least able to stand back up, even though it caused him obvious pain and gave Murky one last look that was almost tender in nature.

Murky understood. Before he could do anything, she flung her arms around his neck and hugged him. "Goodbye," she said through copious tears.

Henderson and Jesse's maneuvers with the grenades must have been doing quite a lot of damage to the creature down in the hole where they couldn't see, because the ant-lion was slipping slowly back in. That didn't stop it from trying to grab a few of the townspeople to take down with it. Before it could reach anyone with its mandibles though, Chicago threw himself into their reach. The ant-lion grabbed on to him and tried to crush him, but the dinosaur slashed at the giant insect's face, tearing up its eyes and causing the thing to howl in pain.

"The charges are set!" Laura called out. "Everyone get out of the way!"

The last few people who hadn't already run dove out of the way for cover. Murky looked away from the flash as the explosives went off. At first she didn't think they had worked, but then the edge of the portal became erratic, and the color of the blue light intensified. The ant-lion gave one last scream of agony then dropped all the way back down the hole.

The blue portal snapped shut with a terrific boom, leaving nothing behind to show that it had ever been there but dirt, rock, and broken pavement.

CHAPTER SIXTEEN

As the buzzing and thrumming that had been caused by the portal died down and echoed off into the night, an uneasy silence fell over Kettle Hollow for several seconds. Then, as one, everyone in the center of town cheered. Or at least, the ones who were still alive did.

The four young friends found each other and made their way through the throngs, looking for anyone in authority that they might be able to speak to. Agent Larson was at the edge of the crowd, her hands on the hips of her now-ragged suit and a smile on her face despite the obvious exhaustion. "I don't know how any of you did it, but I'm not going to deny the results."

Laura looked down at the ground, although she otherwise stood tall. "Are we going to get in trouble then?"

"It's kind of hard to get you in trouble for something that, on the record, never even happened," Larson said.

"So we're not going to be able to tell anyone about any of this?" Laura asked.

"Of course not," Larson said. "If you don't want the government to disappear you somewhere, you're going to need to keep quiet about this for the rest of your life."

"But what about Chicago?" Murky asked. She wiped her cheeks to get rid of some of the tears, but more just replaced them. "He deserves to be remembered for what he did, doesn't he?"

"Uh, who's Chicago?" Agent Larson asked.

"The dinosaur," Laura said. "And yeah, he does. He saved our lives in the end. He probably saved yours, too."

"I suppose there might be something that could be done," Larson said as she looked at the ruined and wrecked mass of earth and concrete that had once been Kettle Hollow's only intersection with a stoplight. "The government is going to have some rebuilding to do if they want to keep the townsfolk quiet. I don't see why we can't put a statue of your friend at the center of it as a memorial. We just couldn't put anything on it explaining why."

"I... I think that would be good," Murky said through a series of sniffles.

"George!" someone yelled from the confusion of townsfolk and soldiers. Henderson turned toward the sound of his given name and saw his father running straight for him. Henderson stiffened like he was afraid his dad was about to yell at him, but instead the man ran right up to his son and hugged him hard.

"I'm so proud of you, George," he said.

"It's Henderson," Henderson said. "I prefer that to George."

His dad pulled back and looked Henderson in the eye. He must have seen something there more grown-up than he'd expected, because he nodded. "When did you start going by that?"

"I've been going by that for a long time, Dad."

"Then that's what I'll call you."

"Agent Larson?" one of the soldiers asked. "What are your orders now?"

"Orders? Why would you be asking for orders from me?" she asked.

The soldier actually looked sheepishly at her. "The general and most of his subordinates were either eaten, crushed or blown up," he said. "You're now the highest-ranking person here, even if you are technically a civilian. For the moment, you're completely in charge of Project Subterranea."

"Then until someone higher up says otherwise, we are shutting everything down," Larson said. "No more attempts to weaponize any of this." She began issuing orders to the remaining military people, having them pull back from the ruined center of town and escort the townspeople to the makeshift camps they had set up around the outside of the town limits. Surprisingly few of the people of Kettle Hollow complained about not being able to go directly home. Those homes would have been ransacked when the ant people came out of the portal to take them, making the houses little more than bad reminders right now of what kind of hellish night they'd all had. Everyone followed the military without question, and many were already nodding along as men in camouflage explained that they were all going to have to agree to a cover story if they wanted to continue the rest of their lives without mysteriously disappearing. Everyone was so lost in their own issues that no one, not even Agent Larson or their parents, noticed that the four kids who had saved them all weren't immediately following.

Laura, Henderson, Jesse, and Murky stood in the ruined street where, twenty-four hours ago, there had been Kettle Hollow's only stoplight, and twenty-four minutes ago there had been a glowing blue portal to some other kind of world.

"You know, it's kind of sad that no one outside of Kettle Hollow is going to ever know this happened," Henderson said.

"Probably can't be helped," Laura said. "If everyone else knew what was possible, and what the government had been doing…"

"No, not that," Henderson said. "I don't care a single rat's fart about that. I mean that no one will ever know that we're the awesome ones who saved everyone. At the very least, Agent Larson should give us a secret medal. Or a million dollars."

"I'm pretty sure I'd prefer the million dollars," Jesse said.

"Yeah. Forget about the medal," Henderson said. "That's lame."

"Maybe we can at least convince them to give us all new bikes," Murky said through her continued sniffles. "Henderson, you might even be able to convince them to give you a Murray X20c."

"Screw that," Henderson said. "If the military is going to reward us, I'm asking for a Skyway T/A. If the government is paying, I might as well go for one of the best, right?"

Finally they followed the rest of the group, laughing and trying to forget for now everything they had just endured. For now, the town of Kettle Hollow was once again deserted.

In the center of it all, in the ruined mess where the single stoplight had once been, a hole about a foot and a half wide opened in the dirt. Unlike the portal that had been there earlier, this one wasn't surrounded by shimmering blue light. It was a perfectly ordinary hole in the dirt, unremarkable in almost every way except for the thing that was now crawling out of it. An ant, roughly two-foot long and with eight legs instead of six, scurried out of the hole and looked around itself as though bewildered and uncertain of where it was. While it didn't walk on its back two pairs of legs, it was clearly not something of this Earth.

It scurried off into the darkness of a midwestern autumn night, surely not to be the cause of any future trouble. After all, it was only an ant.

THE END

Made in the USA
Middletown, DE
08 June 2022

66860287R00094